American
Dreams

"Dad, I'm sorry," Meg quickly added as her mother moved past her. **"I know I shouldn't have—"**

Jack interrupted, in complete agreement. "That's the first right thing you've said all night. You shouldn't have. And it's not happening again, Meg."

Meg nodded, trying to appease his anger. "Dad, I promise. Sam and I will never—," she began.

"You're right, you won't," he said. "Because there's not going to be a you and Sam, or you and Luke, or even you and Roxanne . . . for the rest of the summer."

"What?" Meg asked in disbelief. "What are you talking about?"

"You're grounded," Jack answered simply. "That's what I'm talking about."

"But Dad—," she pleaded.

"And if you keep talking," he added, "you'll be stuck in this house until . . . I don't even know when." Meg looked at her father and knew he was dead serious. Nothing she could say would change anything. She'd never seen him this angry and upset. Especially at her. She spun around and ran up the stairs to her attic room, slamming the door behind her and throwing herself headfirst onto her bed. As if being stuck in the riot and being worried sick about the people she loved weren't punishment enough, now she had to deal with the wrath of her father and being made to feel like a prisoner in her own home.

American Dreams

END OF SUMMER

A novel by Liz Tigelaar based on the television series created
by Jonathan Prince

New York London Toronto Sydney

Simon Spotlight
An imprint of Simon & Schuster Children's Publishing Division
1230 Avenue of the Americas, New York, New York 10020
© 2004 NBC Studios, Inc. and Universal Network Television LLC. *American Dreams*, its characters, and related trademarks and copyrights are the property of NBC Studios, Inc. and Universal Network Television LLC. Licensed by Universal Studios Licensing LLLP.
All rights reserved, including the right of reproduction in whole or in part in any form.

Photo credits: National Broadcasting Company, Inc. and Kevin Foley (front cover) and Paul Drinkwater (back cover)
SIMON SPOTLIGHT and colophon are registered trademarks of Simon & Schuster.
Manufactured in the United States of America
First Edition 10 9 8 7 6 5 4 3 2 1
ISBN 0-689-87081-7

END OF SUMMER

Prologue

"What about Sam?" Meg asked desperately, her blue eyes wide with terror as her uncle Pete ushered her to safety. Meg wasn't sure what was happening. One minute she'd been with Sam at her dad's store, just like normal, then suddenly the city was swarming with rampaging looters and fires were blazing everywhere she looked. "Sam!" Meg yelled, calling to her friend, who was still in the midst of the riot. Her uncle tightened his grip on her arm.

"We can't leave Sam!" Meg shouted to Pete, who wasn't listening. He forced her toward the back of his patrol car, moving her away from a nearby storefront that was in flames. Families were evacuating a five-story apartment building next door, terrified mothers holding on to their children for dear life.

"Get in the car, Meg," Pete ordered.

Meg pleaded with Pete. "But that guy—Nathan's friend's been shot."

"In the car, Meg," Pete shouted. "Now!"

Frantic, Meg looked through the windshield at the scene outside. "Please, Uncle Pete," she begged. "Can't we take Sam with—" He slammed the car door, cutting her off.

She heard a loud crash as a group of men tipped over a parked car. Across the street police used their billy clubs to fend off a group of rowdy teenagers. Meg banged on the rear window, trying to catch Sam's eye. "Sam. SAM!"

Sam was crouched on the sidewalk, pressing a ripped T-shirt over a bleeding wound in Willy Johnson's stomach. Sam's cousin Nathan urged his injured friend not to die, to stay with him until help arrived. As Sam pressed the makeshift compress tighter, his hands trembling with fear, Nathan pleaded with Willy. "Don't give up. You got to fight now."

As Meg banged harder on the car window, desperate to get Sam's attention, more gunshots, followed by screams, echoed across Columbia Avenue. Sam looked up, startled by the noise. After glancing around, trying to find the source of the gunshots, he trained his frightened gaze on Meg in the back of Pete's patrol car. She stared into his eyes with numb disbelief, horrified at the thought of leaving him.

"Sam!" she screamed, both fists pummeling the window as if her life depended on it. "SAM!"

Suddenly the car lurched into drive. "Uncle Pete!" Meg cried, spinning around. "Wait. Please— you can't do this. We can't leave Sam."

"Sam can take care of himself," Pete assured her. "This is his neighborhood." Meg looked at her favorite uncle—the one who had always understood her, who had always made her laugh, the one who she had sometimes wished were her dad because he seemed so much more fun than her own. She saw him in a new light as a wave of anger and disgust washed over her. He was a cop, his job was to protect and serve, but obviously that oath didn't extend to Sam, even though he was Meg's friend and needed their help. Her uncle was no different from the rest of them. He didn't get it either. As the car pulled away Meg felt as if she and Sam were being ripped apart, thrust back into separate worlds—the worlds that conspired to keep them apart despite their friendship.

Meg continued looking out the back window, watching as Sam grew smaller and smaller in the distance. She squinted, trying to make out what was happening. She saw an officer approach Nathan from behind, quickly forcing his hands behind his back. Sam jumped up, ready to defend his cousin, but was pounced on by more police.

"They're attacking Sam!" Meg cried. "Uncle Pete! Tell them to stop," she begged. "Please . . . we have to turn around." Meg leaned forward and grabbed his arm. "Please!"

"Meg!" Pete yelled sternly. "Sit down." Meg could tell by his tone that he wouldn't turn the car around no matter how much she begged and pleaded.

As she watched Sam disappear completely Meg thought back over the last few hours. All she had wanted to do was convince Sam to come to her sweet-sixteen party. Instead they had been caught in a war zone—windows were smashed, stores were looted, fires were started, and people swarmed the streets as the police took rioters into custody. And whereas Sam would have done anything to keep her safe, Meg couldn't even convince her own uncle to help him. She had let Sam down. The image of his terrified face as he knelt on the ground, clutching a blood-soaked T-shirt, burned Meg's eyes and sent tears streaming down her face.

Meg looked out at the streetlights speeding by in blurry streaks and replayed the events of the day in her mind, trying to make sense of what had happened. Although she usually spent her afternoons dancing on *American Bandstand*, she had stayed home today to help her mother with the final preparations for her sweet-sixteen party. While her mom ran last-minute errands for the party, and her younger sister, Patty, was busy watching Martha and the Vandellas perform on television, Meg grabbed Sam's party favor and slipped out the back door. She knew she wasn't supposed to go to North Philly, but she also knew that Sam was working at her father's new electronics store on Girard Avenue—and more importantly, that her dad wasn't there. He'd already caught her going to North Philly once before, and she couldn't risk getting in trouble with him again.

As Meg sat on the bus heading toward North Philly she rehearsed over and over again, like a broken record, what she wanted to tell Sam. He had turned down her birthday invitation, and she knew it wasn't just because he didn't feel comfortable coming to her party. He was turning his back on their friendship, a friendship that had come to mean so much to Meg. She wished she could put into words how much he meant to her. From the outside, she knew, their lives couldn't have looked more dissimilar, but Meg had never had a friend with whom she had so much in common. If people could accept her friendship with Roxanne, who was her polar opposite—loud, bold, and more daring than Meg could ever imagine being—why couldn't they accept her friendship with Sam? Meg knew the reason, deep down. She knew this wasn't about compatibility, that it was about something else. Something nobody wanted to say out loud but everybody thought. It was because Meg was white and Sam was black. But Meg was determined not to let that get in the way of their friendship.

Sometimes Sam couldn't help but be envious of Meg—her life seemed so easy by comparison. She came from a large Irish-Catholic family, with two brothers and a sister. They were by no means rich, but they were at least comfortable. She danced as a regular on Sam's favorite show, *American Bandstand*, and got to rub elbows with singers from Lesley Gore to Marvin Gaye. A couple of times she was even interviewed by Dick Clark. Also, Meg didn't have to worry about kids at school throwing her uniform in the locker room showers or picking on her because her skin was a different color from theirs. And Meg didn't have to listen to constant harassment from Nathan for wanting to fit in, to be just another kid at school, rather than "the colored kid with the track scholarship."

Despite all their differences, Meg and Sam were

alike in ways only they knew about. Only they knew how they both had covered their eyes at the same scary moment in *The Birds*; only they knew how they both loved the Angels and the Kinks and hated Thelonious Monk; only they knew how it felt to be innocently walking home from the movies together only to get stopped and questioned by the police and then screamed at by their fathers. And only they knew how important their friendship truly was—no obstacle, no matter how great, could change that.

On her mission to see Sam, Meg walked nervously down the streets of North Philly. Girard Avenue was eerily quiet. A woman called to her kids out of a third-floor apartment, telling them to get inside. The kids scampered up their front stoop and slammed the door behind them. Meg picked up her pace a little, not sure why she suddenly felt as though she needed to hurry.

As she peered in the window of her father's store she saw Sam diligently preparing for tomorrow's grand opening. His father, Henry, was going to be the manager of the new Pryor's TV and Radio and had enlisted Sam's help in getting the place ready.

Henry had worked for Meg's father, Jack, for years. Around the holidays, when business was slow, Henry had suggested running ads in the predominantly black newspapers to bring in more business. His plan worked, which gave him the confidence to broach another subject with his boss: He suggested opening a second store in his own neighborhood, on Girard Avenue in North Philly. With Sam's help Henry had stayed up all night drafting a letter to Jack, listing all the reasons the second store would be a success. The next day Henry waited nervously for the perfect time to approach Jack, then summoned all his courage and read the letter aloud, his hands shaking the entire time. Jack had always wanted to open a second store, and now just a few months later it seemed both Jack's and Henry's dreams were about to come true. Managing the store was an amazing opportunity not only for Henry, but for the entire Walker family. If anything, it gave Sam hope that his own dreams could come true with a little determination and hard work.

It wasn't until a few moments had passed that Sam, lost in thought, noticed Meg standing on the other side of the glass display window. His heart simultaneously sank and lifted at the sight of her. With the sunlight hitting her hair, she couldn't have looked more angelic and beautiful. She pushed the door open and approached him with a resolve he'd never seen in her before.

"Here," she said, holding out a chocolate record with his name on it. "I want you to have it. Because whether you come to my party or not, it doesn't change anything. You and me . . . we're friends." Sam looked at the record and knew that as much as he tried to deny it—because denying it seemed easier than actually accepting it—Meg was right. They *were* friends. Even if he got frustrated sometimes and took his anger out on her, he valued her friendship more than she knew. He just had a hard time talking to her about things he didn't think she could possibly understand. As he looked down at the chocolate peace offering in her hands Sam was reminded of the fight they'd had a couple days earlier.

They had been taking turns driving with Meg's boyfriend, Luke, when Sam said he had to go soon to make it home by curfew. His was one of the neighborhoods that had been affected by the "citywide" curfew, which was being enforced only in certain areas of Philadelphia.

"That curfew isn't fair," Meg remarked sympathetically. "My uncle Pete says it's the mayor who—"

"Your uncle's a cop," Sam interrupted, his voice filled with a hostility Meg rarely heard.

"What's the difference if my uncle's a cop?" she asked. "Because if you think—"

"You gonna start thinking for me again?" he snapped. "Telling me how you know what I'm feeling?"

Meg tried to explain that she was just upset for him, but Sam wouldn't listen. Her voice rose with her emotion. "Why do you have to act like we're on different sides?" she asked.

"Because we are!" Sam yelled back. But even as he said the words he knew it wasn't her that made him angry; it was everything. It was getting picked on because he was one of a handful of black students in an all-white school. It was having his cousin Nathan constantly preaching to him about black power and coming down on him because of his desire to fit in. It was having to share the sofa bed in the living room with Nathan because the Walkers' apartment wasn't big enough to sleep four people, let alone five. It was a waiter refusing to seat him with Meg in a diner because his kind wasn't welcome there. Everything combined left him feeling so angry and confused.

But now Meg was standing right in front of him,

saying that they were friends and nothing could change that. And suddenly things didn't feel so confusing anymore. In fact, Sam wondered if things could really be this easy. It seemed like in this one moment anything was possible. Dreams that had once seemed to be only dreams had the potential to come true.

Sam reached out and took the record, accepting Meg's gesture. A broad smile slowly appeared on Meg's face. Her eyes lit up, and at that moment she knew everything was right again.

That's when the riot began.

One

"**Y**ou all right, Bandstand?" Pete asked, calling her by his special nickname for her, as he turned around to look at his niece in the backseat. Meg nodded sullenly. They were safely away from the riot, but still she could barely stand to look at her uncle.

Meg had seen her uncle Pete through the chaotic crowd when she and Sam were running toward the Walkers' apartment building. She had watched as he grabbed a young black man from behind, putting his arm around the man's throat.

"That's Nathan," Sam yelled desperately. "Your uncle's got Nathan!" At that moment Willy Johnson grabbed a lead pipe off the ground and lunged for Pete, whose partner acted quickly, pulling out his gun and shooting Willy in the stomach. Meg and Sam stopped suddenly at the sound of the gunshot. They watched as Willy sank to his knees and collapsed on the ground. Meg stared, frozen at the sight, as Sam ran to Willy's side. Pete spun around, his gaze landing on Meg, realizing she had seen the entire thing. Before Meg could even process a single thought, Pete had grabbed her arm and was pulling her toward his car.

"Meg," Pete asked again, "come on . . . say something." Meg snapped back to the present. She looked out the window and realized they were almost home.

"I saw him get shot," she said softly. "Nathan's friend."

Pete defended the actions of his partner. "Nathan is a bad guy, Meg. And his friend Willy Johnson— who do you think started this whole thing?" Seeing Meg's confusion and disbelief, Pete explained matter-of-factly, "He started spreading a story about something that wasn't his business and wasn't even true. He just got everyone in that neighborhood worked up."

"So what . . . you think this whole thing started just because of a rumor?" Meg snapped back.

"I don't just think it, I *know* it," Pete replied. "Some people . . . they're just looking for an excuse to be mad." Not giving an inch, Meg stared out the window, noticing how dark and quiet the street was in her neighborhood. She didn't need an excuse to be mad. She already had about a hundred reasons brewing in her mind, many of which were directed at her uncle.

Pete pulled the car into the Pryors' driveway. "Everything's gonna be fine, Meg. You'll see." Meg continued to stare out of the window, blinking back tears. With Sam out there in the riot, with the world feeling like it was burning down around them, it was hard to believe anything would ever be all right again.

"Come on," he said gently as he put the car in park. "Your mother's been worried sick." Before Meg could fully climb out of the car, her mother was already hugging her tightly.

Helen ushered Meg inside, sitting her down at the kitchen table. "Patty," Helen called. "Put some water on the stove." Meg's younger sister, Patty, was sitting in the den intently watching the riot coverage on TV. She hadn't moved from the spot in hours. Despite being a precocious know-it-all whose goal in life seemed to be to annoy Meg, Patty quickly jumped up at the sight of her older sister and moved to the kitchen.

"Thanks, hon," her mother said as she walked out to the mudroom to talk privately to Pete. Patty busied herself with filling the teapot and putting it on the stove, not quite sure whether to tell Meg how relieved she was that she was safe. As Patty started to speak Meg shushed her, trying to overhear her mom's conversation. Meg strained to listen for any bits and pieces of conversation she could make out. But as she listened something beyond them caught Meg's eye. It was a paper lantern that swayed gently in the breeze.

She realized the backyard was still decorated for her sweet-sixteen party. The oak trees were trimmed with white Christmas lights and colored paper lanterns; white plastic tables borrowed from the church were placed strategically around the yard. Meg thought of all the effort she and Patty had put into the seating arrangements—cousins with cousins, all the tables boy-girl-boy-girl, except one where Sam and her boyfriend, Luke, were supposed to be seated. The extra freezer was filled with scoops of sherbet in hollow coconut shells, and the chocolate records with everyone's names on them sat in tins on the kitchen counter. A few hours ago the party had seemed so important. Now the only thing that mattered was that Sam was still out there in the riot.

Interrupting Meg's drifting thoughts, Patty tentatively asked, "Do you want Ovaltine?"

"Sure," Meg mumbled.

The novelty of Patty acting so nice was making her feel worse rather than better. With everything falling apart outside, for once Meg would have found more comfort in her sister's usual annoying behavior—until Patty whispered, "Mom's been smoking."

"Patty!" Meg responded, exasperated. "Mom doesn't smoke!"

"Uh-huh," Patty answered defiantly. "There's a pack in her sewing kit in the linen closet." Meg was sure Patty was lying. Her mom smoking was hard to imagine. Her best friend, Roxanne, smoked—all the time, in fact—but not Meg's mother. "She smokes one when she's worried," Patty added. "But the whole pack is gone." If Patty was really telling the truth, her mom must have been terrified.

Meg suddenly looked around, realizing that two people were conspicuously absent. "Where are JJ and Dad?" JJ was Meg's older brother, a former high school football star. After getting cut from his college team because of a severe ankle injury, he had made the rash decision to enlist in the marines—a decision that had surprised everyone, including his longtime girlfriend, Beth. Anticipating his departure, they all were still waiting for word from the enlistment office to know where JJ was headed—and when. Patty looked at Meg in disbelief, surprised that she didn't know where JJ and her dad were.

"They're still out there, Meg," Patty answered. Patty could have told Meg about how determined JJ had looked when he left, how Helen had wanted to stop him but had to let him go, how Beth had waited at their house for hours, until her parents came looking for her. Patty could have said that no one in their family would be out in the riot if it weren't for Meg. But she didn't. All she said was, "They went looking for you."

As Meg took this in she heard the back door slam. Uncle Pete was leaving, probably heading back out into the riot. Meg watched as her mother mouthed a prayer and quickly made the sign of the cross. Thinking of JJ and her dad and Sam out there in danger, Meg slowly did the same thing.

"Is the phone working yet?" Meg asked her mom as Helen tucked her into bed. She knew her daughter was too old for that, but given everything that had happened, it just felt right.

"Not yet, hon. The lines are still jammed," her mother answered. "We'll hear from them soon. Don't worry."

Meg responded tentatively, "Aren't you worried?" Now that Patty had mentioned it, Meg could smell the smoke on her mother's hands as she pulled the covers up under Meg's chin.

"No, I'm not," her mother lied. "Everything is going to be fine."

"But what if it's not?" Meg asked, her voice shaking at the thought. "What if something happens to—"

Helen interrupted. "What's going to happen," she explained, "is that your father and brother are going to be home soon."

Meg looked out the bedroom window, avoiding her mother's gaze. "It's all my fault," Meg said softly. And as much as her mother tried to reassure her that it wasn't, she knew it was. No one had forced her to go to North Philly alone. No one had encouraged her not to tell anyone where she was going until it was too late. That was her decision. And now, because of that, her dad and brother were out there trying to find her. Sam was caught in the middle because he had been trying to protect her. If anything happened, it was her fault, and nothing her mother could say would change that.

"Your uncle Pete told me what happened out there," Helen confessed. "Where you were, what you saw." Meg nodded, not ready to talk about it yet. The image of Willy Johnson getting shot played over and over in her mind.

"You're lucky he was there," Helen said. "Your uncle. He cares a lot about you."

"Don't defend him, Mom!" Meg responded, frustrated. "You don't even know what happened."

Helen put her hand on her daughter's arm. "Then, tell me," she said gently.

"He left Sam," Meg answered. "He left him there in the middle of that mess with someone dying in his arms."

"Meg, I'm sure your uncle had—," Helen began.

Meg interrupted, realizing her mom would never understand. "You weren't there. You didn't see it, Mom."

Helen understood, and there was nothing she could say or do to change how Meg felt. All she could do was hold her daughter's hand, offering any comfort she could, until Meg slowly, finally, drifted off to sleep.

It was well after midnight when Meg heard the front door open and close. At the sound of JJ's voice she threw off her covers and hurried down the attic stairs. He was heading into his bedroom.

"JJ," she called, running over to him and throwing her arms around his neck.

He sighed, relieved. "Thank God you're here. We looked everywhere."

"I know," Meg responded quickly. She and JJ were talking so fast they were overlapping. "Dad told me to stay put, but—"

JJ interrupted. "Dad said you were at the Girard store—"

"We were," Meg answered. "But—"

JJ continued, talking over her. "When we got there—"

"Meg!" a voice yelled sternly. Meg looked over the upstairs banister at her dad, who stood at the bottom of the stairs. She expected him to run and pick her up, engulfing her in a big bear hug, relieved at the sight of her—but instead . . .

"What the *hell* were you thinking?" his loud voice boomed. Helen reached out and put her hand on his arm, hoping to calm him.

"Jack," Helen whispered. "This isn't the—"

"Out there, in North Philly?" Jack interrupted. "By yourself?" This was hardly the response Meg had anticipated. But knowing her dad, she realized she had been naive to think he would just let her trip to North Philly go without punishment.

Meg corrected him. "I wasn't by myself." She hesitated for a moment. "I was . . . with Sam."

Jack threw his hands up in mock relief. "And that's supposed to make me feel better?" Jack asked. "You defied me, Meg."

"No I didn't!" argued Meg, knowing as she said it she was making the situation worse. "You never said I couldn't go to the Girard store," Meg added.

"Don't give me that, Meg," Jack spit. "You know better. When're you gonna start using your head for once?"

Meg pleaded with Jack. "You don't understand. I just wanted to bring him his record—"

"You risked your life out in that riot for what?" Jack shouted. "A stupid record?"

Meg's eyes stung, filling with tears. "It wasn't stupid to me!" she cried.

"There was a riot going on!" Jack shouted.

Meg defended herself. "I didn't know that!"

"That's right," Jack snapped. "Because, despite what you might believe, you don't know everything."

"JJ!" Will cried happily. The yelling had woken Meg's younger brother, Will, and he made his way into the hall in his pajamas. Will, who had suffered from polio and walked with a limp, had haphazardly tried to buckle his leg brace on his own, and it wasn't quite secure.

"Will," Helen said sternly. "Back to bed."

"Hey, Thrill," JJ said, picking him up and throwing him over his shoulder. Will laughed as JJ took him into his room. Not even Will's happiness at seeing JJ could lighten the situation. Meg took a deep breath.

"Dad, I'm sorry," Meg quickly added as her mother moved past her. "I know I shouldn't have—"

Jack interrupted, in complete agreement. "That's the first right thing you've said all night. You shouldn't have. And it's not happening again, Meg."

Meg nodded, trying to appease his anger. "Dad, I promise. Sam and I will never—," she began.

"You're right, you won't," he said. "Because there's not going to be a you and Sam, or you and Luke, or even you and Roxanne . . . for the rest of the summer."

"What?" Meg asked in disbelief. "What are you talking about?"

"You're grounded," Jack answered simply. "That's what I'm talking about."

"But Dad—," she pleaded.

"And if you keep talking," he added, "you'll be stuck in this house until . . . I don't even know when." Meg looked at her father and knew he was dead serious. Nothing she could say would change anything. She'd never seen him this angry and upset. Especially at her. She spun around and ran up the stairs to her attic room, slamming the door behind her and throwing herself headfirst onto her bed. As if being stuck in the riot and being worried sick about the people she loved weren't punishment enough, now she had to deal with the wrath of her father and being made to feel like a prisoner in her own home.

After a moment there was a knock at the door.

"Go away," Meg yelled, muffled through the pillow. The door opened anyway. JJ appeared.

JJ offered a quiet comment. "He's not mad at you," he said.

"Is that why he grounded me?" Meg spit back. JJ sat down on the edge of her bed.

"It's not about you, Meg," he added.

"It sure felt like it when he was screaming at me," Meg answered.

JJ sighed. "You should have seen it out there. You have no idea."

"No idea?" Meg laughed incredulously. Was JJ kidding? She had been stuck in the middle of the riot, watching people being beaten with clubs. She had seen her uncle attack Sam's cousin, and his partner shoot Nathan's friend. "I know exactly what happened out there. In fact, I can't get it out of my—"

JJ interrupted, keeping his voice low. "The store's gone. The Girard store burned down."

"What?" Meg asked, shocked. She sat up, wiping tears from her eyes with the back of her hand. "What do you mean 'gone'?"

"I mean, it's over, Meg," JJ answered simply. "It's over."

As the words sank in Meg felt like the world that had been spinning so fast suddenly came to a grinding halt. The store was gone. Meg couldn't believe it. That store represented the hopes and dreams of both her father and Sam's father, and in a way, the hopes and dreams of their families as well. Now, just like that, everything they'd worked so hard for was gone—the burned-out, looted store on Girard Avenue, Meg's friendship with Sam . . . gone. It had taken them so much time and effort to get there, and now, in an instant, a spark in North Philly had ignited a fire that left only ashes and shattered dreams behind.

Two

Meg stood outside the charred facade of the Girard store, overwhelmed at the sight. The PRYOR'S TV AND RADIO sign had fallen to the ground and split in half, lying broken on the sidewalk. With the sunlight beaming down, the glass that covered the pavement and crunched beneath her feet looked like crystal snow. The street was quiet and strangely empty, but with the heat just starting to creep up on the day and the birds chirping in the distance, she could almost be fooled into thinking it was just like any other morning in late August . . . except it wasn't. It was the day after the riot. And to Meg it felt like nothing would be the same again.

Meg stepped over the cracked sign and pushed the door open. It was hanging on by only one hinge. The front windows were broken, the inside of the store looted, the merchandise gone. The big consoles were tipped over and destroyed, while the narrow shelves that were once lined with small televisions and radios sat empty. Meg stared at the mess in disbelief. All her father's hard work, all of Henry's hard work, all of Sam's hard work—gone in an instant. Meg felt helpless amid the debris.

Suddenly she spun around, feeling as if she was being watched. She gasped at the sight of Nathan, who stood in the doorway. His hat was pulled down, almost covering his eyes, but Meg could feel him looking her up and down. He shook his head slowly from side to side. Frightened, Meg backed away, coming to the slow realization that she had nowhere to go. She could feel her knees knocking together underneath her plaid skirt. Despite the summer heat outside, the room suddenly felt icy.

"Didn't learn your lesson yesterday, Goldilocks?" Nathan chided as he stepped inside, revealing he wasn't alone.

Behind him stood Willy Johnson, holding the same lead pipe he had tried to use on Uncle Pete the night before. Meg inhaled quickly at the sight of Willy, feeling as if the air were suddenly being sucked out of the room. She felt short of breath and light-headed.

"I—I thought—you were . . . ," Meg stuttered, trying to find the words. "I saw you—you got shot."

Willy smiled a twisted smile as his voice lulled, smooth and calm like music. "I'm fine now, girl," he said. "You think a bullet's gonna keep me down?" In a sudden motion Willy grabbed the pipe with both hands and swung it like a baseball bat into the middle of a television console. Meg screamed at the sound of it shattering.

"Please," she cried. "Stop!" Desperate and panicked, she tried to think of anything to say. "Sam—he'll be here," she lied, trying to keep her shaking voice steady. "Any minute. He's meeting me—here." Nathan and Willy laughed.

Nathan scoffed, "You think Sam's gonna be your knight in shining armor?"

Willy added menacingly, moving closer to Meg, "He's no *white* knight, that's for sure." Meg backed up, until she hit the wall. Willy reached out and touched her blond hair; Meg's eyes were full of fear.

"Please don't hurt me," she pleaded. "I swear . . . Sam'll be here, and he won't let you—"

"Sam is dead," Willy barked, interrupting her. "He's not gonna be here or anywhere else." Meg steadied herself, feeling as if she'd been cut off at the knees.

"What?" Meg whispered, her heart breaking. "No, that's not true. You're lying," she said, her eyes filling with tears. "Sam's alive . . . he's . . ." Meg broke down, sobbing. Willy grabbed her by her shoulders, shaking her.

"Sam's dead," he yelled. "And it's your fault, Meg." He shook her harder, as if she were a rag doll, her body limp, shouting her name as if it were a curse word or an accusation. "Meg! Meg!"

"Meg," she heard a voice say. "Meg . . . Meg!"

Startled, Meg opened her eyes. Roxanne was leaning over her, shaking her. Meg sat up and looked around, confused. She wasn't standing in the Girard store being threatened by Nathan and Willy Johnson. She wasn't listening to Willy tell her that Sam was dead. She was at home in her attic. Sun was beaming down through the window above her, a breeze was coming in, and her best friend was standing above her with a cigarette in one hand. It all had been a terrible nightmare.

"I've been trying to wake you up for ten minutes," Roxanne complained. Roxanne quickly pulled her in for a big hug. "Happy birthday, Meg!" she said excitedly. "Happy sweet sixteen!" Her birthday? Meg had almost forgotten. Today she was sixteen. Suddenly Meg's heart skipped a beat. Maybe, Meg thought for a moment, the riot was nothing but a terrible dream.

But then it all came rushing back. The party invitation, going to the Girard store to see Sam, being caught in the middle of the riot—it was worse than a nightmare. It was real.

"I tried to call you last night, about the party," Roxanne explained. "But the lines were tied up. My mom was working all night." Roxanne's mom was a telephone operator who often worked nights and weekends, and Roxanne's dad . . . he wasn't really in the picture. "I was stuck at WFIL with Michael Brooks until late," Roxanne continued with her lengthy explanation. "Luckily we broke into *Bonnie Pratt's Pratt-ical Cooking* set and found day-old meatloaf. And let me just say, for having a cooking show, that woman *cannot* cook."

"I'm so happy to see you," Meg said, relieved, her voice still hoarse from screaming the night before. "I was so scared, Roxanne. I thought . . . I thought I might never see you again. . . ."

Roxanne was unsure how to read Meg's outpouring of emotion. "Meg, I was fine. I'm sorry I didn't come by. I assumed the party was cancelled. . . ."

"No, Rox . . . I mean, yes . . . ," Meg began, realizing Roxanne didn't understand. "I mean, yes. The party was cancelled. But I didn't get home until late."

Roxanne was floored. "Don't tell me your dad actually let you out with Luke with that riot going on?" Roxanne asked.

Meg struggled to find the words. "Rox," Meg explained. "That riot? I was in it."

Roxanne gasped. "Meg, you're kidding, right?" The serious look on Meg's face said she wasn't.

"I wish I were," Meg sighed. "Rox . . . you can't even imagine. . . ." Meg trailed off as the images of the night before came flooding back: Willy throwing a television to the ground in the store; a brick flying through the window; Sam running with her through the streets; Uncle Pete grabbing Nathan; Willy getting shot; the way he sank to the ground, bleeding and in pain; Uncle Pete ripping her away from Sam and forcing her to leave him in the midst of the angry mob. Meg shuddered at the thoughts rushing back to her. Roxanne sat down on the corner of the bed, shocked.

"Meg," she said slowly. "Tell me everything." Meg took a deep breath and slowly filled Roxanne in on everything that had happened since she'd seen her last.

When Meg and Roxanne finally came down for breakfast, they were greeted with more enthusiasm than Meg had expected, given how things had ended with her father the night before. The decorations from outside had been taken down, the white plastic tables and chairs put away, but the kitchen was cheerful and festive. In the center of the kitchen table sat a small bouquet of flowers that Patty had cut from the front yard of their mean neighbor, Mrs. Kirby, and in between the kitchen and the den hung a homemade HAPPY BIRTHDAY, MEG sign that Will had labored over for days. Helen stood over the griddle making a big batch of pancakes, spelling out the letters of Meg's name with the batter. When she saw Meg, she quickly approached her, kissing her on the cheek.

"Happy birthday, hon," Helen said, smiling warmly.

Meg appreciated her mom's kindness. "Thanks, Mom."

"Roxanne," Helen asked, "you'll join us for breakfast, right?" Helen knew full well that Roxanne was staying. She never missed an opportunity to eat with the Pryor family.

Roxanne shrugged, acting like it didn't matter either way, when in reality she'd purposefully set her alarm clock early in order to be over by breakfast time. "If you insist," she replied.

"*I* insist," Meg said as she threaded her arm through Roxanne's, grateful that her best friend had come to see her. Especially today.

"Hi, Roxanne!" called Patty from the den. Patty was once again parked in front of the television, watching the continuing riot news coverage.

"Hey, Patty," Roxanne responded. The two girls had a special bond, Roxanne often acting like more of a big sister to Patty than Meg did. Meg reasoned that because Roxanne didn't have any siblings, Patty didn't get on her nerves as much. The mudroom door opened and slammed as JJ entered, carrying in wrapped gifts from the garage.

"Hey, Roxanne," JJ said casually.

Roxanne did a double take, surprised to see him. "JJ!" she exclaimed. "What're you doing home?" Roxanne looked at Meg, confused, but Meg quickly elbowed Roxanne in the side, signaling Roxanne not to ask any more questions. Roxanne got the hint.

"Ow!" Roxanne yelped. She looked at Meg. "That hurt."

Patty called into the kitchen, "They put another curfew in place for tonight."

"Really?" JJ asked as he set the gifts down on the kitchen counter. "'Cause I gotta go to Beth's later."

"Your father wants everyone to stay home today," Helen reminded him.

"Mom," JJ laughed. "If I can handle the marines . . . I think can handle myself out there on the main line."

"The marines?" Roxanne questioned, not realizing what a touchy subject it was. Meg elbowed Roxanne again. "Ow!"

Helen focused on pouring the perfect *G* onto the griddle, not acknowledging JJ's comment.

"Mom," JJ pressed. "I can."

"JJ enlisted," Patty reported to Roxanne. "Because he got cut from the football team at Lehigh—"

"Patty!" Meg admonished. "Shut up!"

"Meg," Helen snapped, her birthday kindness suddenly replaced with her anger that her son was enlisting. "Don't talk to your sister that way. And Patty—mind your own business."

"Wait," Roxanne said to JJ, taking it all in. "You got cut from the team? And *enlisted*?"

JJ headed for the refrigerator and grabbed a bottle of milk out of it. Just as he held the bottle up to his lips to take a sip Helen stopped him.

"Glass," she said without even looking. Reprimanded, JJ opened the cupboard for a glass.

Roxanne said wistfully, "First a football star, now

a man in uniform . . . Beth is one lucky girl." As he poured the milk JJ half smiled, embarrassed.

"Convince Beth of that," Meg joked. "She wasn't too happy at the news."

"Can you blame her?" Helen asked.

"Mom——," JJ began, ready to defend his decision.

His mother cut in. "You two had plans," she said simply.

JJ shrugged, not wanting to fight about it. "Plans change, Mom." His mother had made it clear how she felt about his enlisting. Saying she wasn't happy was an understatement—she was devastated. She'd been ecstatic that JJ was going to college—not for football, but for an education. "Beth understands that. Why can't—"

"Who wants pancakes?" Helen interrupted, ending the discussion with JJ. Meg shot a sidelong glance at her brother, who downed his milk in one large gulp.

Will hurried into the kitchen from the hall. "I do!" JJ picked him up and spun him around. "Faster," Will yelled happily. "Faster, JJ!"

"They're afraid there might be more rioting tonight," Patty called from the den.

"Patty, turn that off," Helen demanded. "And JJ, put your brother down." Patty rolled her eyes and turned off the television, while JJ reluctantly set Will down.

"But I wanted to go faster," Will complained.

JJ tousled his hair. "Later, Thrill," he said.

"We're eating," Helen announced.

"I'm going out to the garage," JJ said, casually reaching for a piece of bacon and popping it in his mouth.

"Now?" Helen asked.

JJ shrugged. "Thought I'd lift some weights. Gotta keep up with the other guys in boot camp."

Roxanne's ears perked up. "Other guys?" she asked, smiling. "As in cute, available other guys?"

"As in out-of-town other guys," JJ laughed.

"Where'd you say you were going to be?" asked Roxanne quickly.

"I didn't," JJ said. Smiling, he grabbed his jacket off the back of the chair and headed out through the mudroom for the garage. "Happy birthday, Meg," he said, realizing he hadn't said it yet.

"What about breakfast?" called Meg. "Mom already made two Js."

JJ muttered, "I lost my appetite."

"Can I eat the Js?" Will pleaded as the mudroom door slammed behind JJ. "Mom? Please?"

With JJ gone Meg realized someone else was

conspicuously absent from her birthday breakfast. "Where's Dad?" Meg asked casually, trying to cover her concern.

"He's at the Girard store," Patty answered simply. "He said he had a lot of work to do, but if you ask me—"

"Nobody did," Meg reminded her.

Patty continued, undeterred. "I think maybe he's not here because he's still mad at you."

"Patty!" Meg said in disbelief. But when Patty turned around, Meg bit her lip nervously. Her dad choosing not to be there for her birthday breakfast couldn't be a good sign. In the hallway the phone rang.

"I'll get it," Patty and Meg yelled simultaneously as they ran for the phone.

"Hello?" Patty answered enthusiastically, beating Meg to the receiver. Disappointed, she handed Meg the phone. "It's for you," she remarked glumly. "It's that producer from *Bandstand*." Meg grabbed the receiver from her sister as Roxanne ran over. Both girls put their ear up to the phone.

"Hello?" Meg said. Michael Brooks explained that he was calling every regular dancer on *Bandstand* to let them know the show was going on as usual, but there was no rush to come back.

"Ask him who's on *Bandstand* today," Roxanne whispered. Meg nodded to Roxanne, still trying to listen to Michael.

"Take your time," Michael said. "Come back and dance when you're ready. When you feel safe."

"Thanks, Michael," Meg responded. "But me and Roxanne—we'll be there."

"Great," Michael said. "Oh, and Meg . . . one more thing."

"Yeah?" Meg asked.

"Happy birthday," he said. Meg smiled, touched that Michael, a producer on one of the most popular shows on television, would remember her birthday.

"Thanks," she answered shyly. Roxanne, getting a little jealous, nudged Meg in the side. "Oh!" Meg said, remembering. "Michael, who's on *Bandstand* today?"

"The Shirelles," Michael said. Roxanne and Meg screamed simultaneously and hung up the phone.

Roxanne hugged Meg happily. "Your birthday just got a whole lot better."

"Definitely," Meg agreed. Realizing what it meant that the phone lines were clear, she said, "Wait—I can call Sam now!" She quickly reached for the phone, but something stopped her. Though she was poised to call, she suddenly felt frozen.

Roxanne noticed Meg's sudden hesitation. "What's wrong? What are you waiting for?"

Meg wasn't sure. She'd been waiting for the phone lines to clear all morning, and now that they were working again, she was scared to call. Deep down she was scared the truth would be something she couldn't handle. What if what Willy Johnson said in her dream was true? What if Sam had been hurt in the riot? Or worse . . . killed? Meg took a deep breath and reached for the phone. She had to make sure Sam was okay.

As the front door swung open a voice boomed, "Helen!" Startled, Meg dropped the phone. Her dad stood in the doorway, already looking agitated. Looking from Meg to Roxanne, Jack knew something was going on—he just wasn't quite sure what. Meg tried to cover the guilty expression on her face, knowing her father wouldn't approve of her calling Sam.

Helen called from the kitchen, "In here!" Jack shut the front door and headed for the kitchen.

"Hi, Dad," Meg said hesitantly, giving him a nervous wave as he passed. She hadn't seen him since he grounded her the night before.

Roxanne smiled sweetly. "Hi, Mr. Pryor," she said, waving. Jack barely acknowledged her. Meg, rolling her eyes, looked at Roxanne. "See?" she mouthed.

"Meg?" Jack said, turning around halfway down the hallway, catching Meg making a face behind his back. Meg snapped to attention. "Happy birthday," he said gently.

Meg smiled, relieved. "Thanks, Dad."

"Meg, Roxanne," Helen called from the kitchen. "Breakfast is ready." Meg looked down at the receiver. Her call to Sam would have to wait. Silently she said a prayer that he was sitting in his apartment in North Philly, eating his breakfast as well.

Three

After her pancakes and presents Meg's spirits were lifted. She and her dad seemed to be getting along. Not only had he eaten her M pancake just to be playful, he'd given her a beautiful charm bracelet for her sixteenth birthday. And as if that weren't enough, she received a new skirt and sweater from her mom, a Beatles album from JJ, a new shade of ballet pink lipstick from Patty, and a glass jar of candy from Will that had SWEETS FOR THE SWEET neatly written on the side.

"My present is coming," Roxanne assured her. "But Luke needs to be there."

Meg gave Roxanne a suspicious look. "What does Luke have to do with it?" she asked, dying to know.

Roxanne shrugged innocently and smiled. "You'll see," she said. "I know! We'll go to the Vinyl Crocodile after *Bandstand* today. Luke and I can give you your present then." Meg clapped her hands excitedly, trying to imagine what it was.

"No way," Jack said sternly, shaking his head.

Meg looked at her father, worried. "What?" she asked hesitantly, shooting a glance at Roxanne.

"You're not leaving this house, Meg. I already told you."

Meg shook her head in disbelief. *So much for a fun breakfast,* she thought. It was back to business as usual in the Pryor house.

"Dad!" Meg gasped. He couldn't be serious. On today of all days, on her sixteenth birthday, she couldn't see her boyfriend, she couldn't dance on *Bandstand.* She couldn't even pick up the phone to see if Sam was all right!

"We went over this last night," Jack reminded her.

"But it's *Bandstand*!" Meg reasoned. "*Bandstand's* different."

Jack shook his head, not wanting to get into it with Meg, but not being able to help himself. "I was just down there," Jack told her. "On Girard—"

"But WFIL is nowhere near Girard!" Meg argued. Jack looked at Helen, wanting some support.

"Meg," Helen said softly. "Your father's right."

"You always take his side!" Meg yelled.

Patty chimed in. "The riot is still going on," she pointed out. "They just said on the news that they doubled the police in North Philly to twelve hundred."

"Shut up, Patty!" Meg ordered.

"Mayor Tate's giving a press conference at noon," Patty continued. "They're afraid more people are coming out—"

"Patty," Meg screamed. "Shut up!"

"Meg!" Helen reprimanded. "I told you—"

"But Mom," Meg complained. "It's not fair!"

"Who said life was fair, Meg?" Jack asked, exasperated.

"But the Shirelles are on *Bandstand* today!" explained Meg. "I can't miss it."

"I don't care if Elvis is on," Jack answered. "You're not going."

Meg stood up from the table, shoving her chair out of the way. "But it's my birthday!" she cried.

Jack stood up too. "Meg," he said, pointing his finger at her, "you should have thought of that yesterday before going down to Girard by yourself!"

"JJ's so lucky," she shouted as she ran down the hallway and up to her room. "He's getting out of here!"

"Teenagers can be *very* difficult," Roxanne sympathized as Patty tried to stifle a laugh. Helen and Jack weren't amused.

Meg locked herself in her bedroom for the rest of the morning and most of the afternoon. She couldn't believe her father. Once again he had proved he didn't understand. Meg suspected that her father had grown up in some weird alternate universe in which he had gone straight from being a kid to being an adult, skipping over his teenage years completely. How else could he have no empathy for what it felt like to be sixteen? He acted like his decision was about keeping her safe, but she knew it was really a punishment. It had always been like that with her dad. He didn't seem to get the fact that she was growing up. She was sixteen now, and she wasn't a little girl anymore. She could make her own decisions and clean up her own messes. Sometimes he laid down so many rules, it was impossible not to break them. Meanwhile, JJ could do whatever he wanted.

Over the past year Meg couldn't believe what JJ had gotten away with. One time JJ blew off a dinner with a Notre Dame coach and got drunk with his best friend, Tommy. Meg was sure he would be grounded for life, but aside from a horrible argument, JJ wasn't punished at all. And another time, when he and Beth had broken up for a little while, JJ stayed out all night with Colleen, the country club waitress, and Jack practically patted JJ on the back! But when Meg went to a *church*, no less, to hear Luke play the piano at a concert, she got grounded for a week. Granted, the church was in North Philly . . . but still, it wasn't fair.

And it wasn't just those two instances of the double standard of Jack's rules. There were many more, even as recently as a few weeks ago, when Patty told Meg a secret that no one was supposed to know. Patty had overheard Jack and Pete talking in the garage. When their entire family had taken their annual summer trip to the Jersey Shore and JJ had decided to stay home to train for Lehigh, Jack had come home to find Beth standing in the kitchen dressed only in JJ's oversize nightshirt, clearly having spent the night. When Patty told Meg about what had happened, Meg was floored. If Jack had caught Meg and Luke in that position, with Meg dressed only in one of Luke's shirts, Meg would definitely be grounded, or maybe even kicked out of the house! And she certainly wouldn't ever be seeing Luke again. Of course at this rate, with her dad still mad at her, she wouldn't see Luke again anyway. The scene she had created at breakfast probably didn't help her cause.

Roxanne left shortly after Meg's outburst, promising to call after *Bandstand* and tell her about meeting the Shirelles. With Roxanne gone, Meg gloomily wallowed in the feeling that this was the worst birthday she could remember. Although dancing on *Bandstand* or seeing Luke would help tremendously, what she really needed was to know that Sam was all right. However, between birthday wishes and out-of-town relatives calling after seeing the nightly news coverage of the riot, the phone was ringing off the hook. All Meg could do was be patient and wait for her father to leave.

Around four o'clock Meg finally decided to leave her room to watch *Bandstand*. As she entered the den the show was about to begin. Patty was sitting right in front of the television set, watching as Dick Clark was introduced.

"And here's the star of our show," the announcer boomed. "Dick Clark!" As the slightly smaller than usual audience applauded in the bleachers she heard the familiar sound of "Bandstand Boogie," indicating the beginning of the show.

"Your big head's blocking the TV," Meg complained. "Move!"

"Your head's bigger than mine," Patty shot back.

"Maybe it's because I'm smarter," Meg offered.

Patty looked at her disdainfully. "Actually, head size has nothing to do with the size or capacity of the brain, Meg," she said. "If you were smarter, you'd know that."

"Patty, shut up." Meg collapsed onto the couch, feeling completely dejected. Not even yelling at Patty could cheer her up. She had hoped watching *Bandstand* would make her feel better, but after seeing Roxanne dancing on the floor with the Shirelles, she felt much worse. She imagined what a great birthday it would have been—to meet the Shirelles, to dance with the Shirelles, to get an autographed record from the Shirelles. It would have been incredible. Especially because she'd never celebrated a birthday while being a regular dancer on *Bandstand*. But she knew that Michael Brooks would have given her a cupcake with a candle in it and wished her a very happy birthday, maybe even giving her a kiss on the cheek. Sure, she had Luke to kiss, but a kiss from Michael Brooks—considering he was, well, Michael Brooks—was pretty special. However, Roxanne, being the considerate, helpful best friend she always was—and given her enormous crush on Michael—would probably have happily offered to be Meg's replacement for the cupcake, the candle, *and* the kiss.

Turning away from the TV, Meg asked Patty cautiously, "Where's Dad?"

Patty shrugged. "How should I know?" she said.

Meg stood up and peered out of the kitchen window into the driveway. The Pryor TV and Radio truck was gone, as was the family station wagon. Meg realized this was her chance to call Sam.

With Patty distracted watching *Bandstand,* Meg crept into the hallway and slowly picked up the phone. Having memorized Sam's number long ago, she dialed the numbers on the rotary phone. She felt like she'd swallowed a dozen butterflies. Her heart raced as the phone rang . . . and rang . . . and rang. Finally, after what felt like an eternity, a man's voice answered. "Hello?"

"Sam!" Meg said too quickly. "It's me."

"I'm sorry," the voice said, sounding weary and tired. "Who is this?"

And Meg realized it wasn't Sam. It was Henry, Sam's dad. Meg stood speechless, unsure of what to say or whether to say anything at all.

"Um . . . ," she said, thinking.

"Is this Meg?" Henry asked. "Meg Pryor?" She wanted to say something, to ask if Sam was all right, but she was afraid her father would find out she'd called the Walkers' apartment. Quickly she slammed down the receiver.

• • •

Meg barely looked up from the book she was reading when Helen walked in with two bags of groceries. *Bandstand* was over, and Meg was feeling more depressed than ever. She even wished that school had started, because a birthday at school would have been better than a birthday at home. At least at school she would have been able to see Roxanne and Luke and Sam all day. After a day stuck in the house even the mean nuns, like Sister Mister, would have been a welcome sight.

"Hi, hon," Helen said cheerily. "How was your day?"

How was your day? Meg thought. *Is she serious?* She continued to stare at the page she'd been reading, but the words and sentences blurred in front of her as her eyes teared up. Helen's heart sank as she took in Meg's reaction. This wasn't the birthday they had painstakingly planned.

It had been Meg's idea to have a Hawaiian luau for her sweet-sixteen party, and because Meg was born at exactly 12:04 A.M., Roxanne had suggested having it the night before her actual birthday so that when 12:04 A.M. hit, they'd be celebrating the exact moment she turned sixteen.

"Sixteen is a monumental milestone," Roxanne had explained to Meg, "that has to be celebrated accordingly." Meg had been counting down the days since her fifteenth birthday. Sixteen was huge because sixteen meant driver's license, and driver's license meant car, and car meant freedom—and freedom was the key to any sixteen-year-old's happiness.

Being stuck in the house all day really made Meg appreciate the concept of freedom. She thought of what she'd seen on the news, people marching through states and to national monuments all in the name of freedom. She felt grateful that all she had to do was pass a driver's test for hers. Although right now the word *freedom* seemed like a foreign concept.

"Oh, no," Helen complained, putting away the groceries. "I forgot eggs. I'm going to have to go back to the store." Meg continued to read, not really interested in eggs or any other food product her mother might have forgotten.

"Meg?" Helen asked. "Maybe I could drop you off at the record shop while I run to the store." Meg's ears perked up and her eyes lit up at the mention of the Vinyl Crocodile. She looked at her mother for confirmation that she meant it.

"Mom . . . ," Meg said, her heart skipping a beat. "Really?"

"Yes, really," Helen told her. "But let's hurry. I have to get dinner started soon."

Meg jumped up and threw her arms around her mother's neck. "Mom, thank you! Thank you so much," she exclaimed, elated.

As Meg hurriedly followed her mother out to the car Helen took her hand.

"Let's not tell your father," she whispered conspiratorially.

A broad smile stretched across Meg's face as she nodded her head vigorously. She promised her mom that it would be their little secret.

Four

"Twenty minutes," Helen reminded Meg as her daughter leaped out of the passenger-side door before the car had come to a complete stop.

Meg slammed the door. "Okay!" she called, running toward the record store.

"Meg!" Helen shouted out of the open window. Meg spun around, running backward. She didn't want to waste a single precious moment of her freedom.

"What?" she yelled, somewhat annoyed. She wished her mom would go run her errand and stop shouting things out of the car window.

"Meet me right back here . . . ," Helen said sternly. "Twenty minutes?"

"Okay!" Meg shouted back, not even looking at her mom as she tore down the steps. She burst through the front door of the Vinyl Crocodile. Startled, Luke, her boyfriend of nine months, looked up from shelving records.

"Meg!" he said happily. With the threat of more rioting hanging in the air, she had been the only person to walk into the store in the last two hours. It seemed that no one in Philly was in the mood to buy records today. He hurried over to her, wrapping his arms around her in a big hug. Meg was taken aback. This outpouring of affection wasn't typical Luke behavior.

"I was so worried about you," Luke said. "Your mom called me last night looking for you. . . ."

"I know," Meg said apologetically. She took a deep breath, preparing to launch into the entire story again despite an overwhelming sense of dread at the prospect of retelling it—how scared she'd been, how alone she'd felt, how worried she still was about Sam. But with only twenty short minutes to be with Luke, she wanted to focus on the present, not rehash the past.

"Roxanne called me after she left your house this morning," Luke informed her. "She told me everything."

A wave of relief washed over Meg, who was happy to talk about anything other than the riot. "Thank you, Luke," she said, her voice full of gratitude. Luke grabbed her hand, thrilled to see her standing right in front of him. Meg couldn't help but smile seeing how worried Luke was and how much he cared.

She remembered her first encounter with Luke last November at the Vinyl Crocodile, when twice he'd slipped a Bob Dylan record into her bag instead of the Shangri-Las albums she'd paid for. At the time it had both infuriated and intrigued her. She remembered how upset Luke had been, although he refused to admit it, when her first kiss was on TV with her former *Bandstand* dance partner, Jimmy Riley, instead of him. She remembered how happy she had felt when Luke finally kissed her, outside her church on Christmas Eve. She remembered how disappointed she'd been at the Valentine's Day dance when she realized that she and Luke were too different to be a good couple, and how broken-hearted she'd been when Luke was the first to say it aloud. And after weeks and weeks of trying to forget about Luke, she remembered, she went to him, grabbed his face, and told him to shut up. Then, to Luke's surprise, she planted a huge kiss on him. She realized in that moment that despite their differences, Luke was the boy she wanted to be with. In the nine months they'd been dating, they'd never told each other "I love you." But though she'd never heard the words, Meg felt as though Luke really did love her. Not that she would mind hearing him say it, especially today, on her sixteenth birthday. In fact, she thought to herself, it was actually the perfect day for him to say—

"Happy birthday," he said lovingly. Meg smiled. *Right, happy birthday,* she thought. He could save the "I love you" for another day.

"Have you spoken with Sam?" he asked, concerned. At the mention of Sam, Meg's eyes welled with tears. Luke was the first who'd asked that question, the only person who seemed to realize how much Sam meant to her. And strangely, he was the person who would have had the most right to object to Meg's friendship with another boy, though Luke consistently remained the most understanding.

Luke and Sam were good friends. Luke played piano for the choir at Sam's church and had even cheered Sam on at a few of his track meets last spring. Once, Meg and Luke showed up at a blues concert and found Sam there with his girlfriend, Anita. It turned out both Luke and Anita loved the blues—a genre of music that Meg and Sam had no interest in whatsoever. Luckily the concert was at the Vinyl Crocodile, so Meg and Sam were able to excuse themselves politely and sneak into the

listening booth to hear music they liked. Meg found
out that Sam liked the Dave Clark Five as much as
she did.

Shortly after that she and Sam started meeting
after school to trade and listen to each other's records
in the listening booth; their record club was born.
They had invited Luke to join, but not even large
headphones could block out Luke's constant scoffing
at their taste in music. Instead he just slipped them
the latest records, and even some that weren't
released yet. He let them hang out in the booth for
hours even though there was a loosely enforced time
limit. Luke had gone so far out of his way for them
that he asked his boss, Mr. Greenwood, if he could
borrow his car to teach Meg and Sam how to drive.
It was during that driving lesson that Luke witnessed
the curfew fight between Meg and Sam, and it was
Luke who comforted her after Sam left her crying.
Luke, of all people, understood how important her
friendship with Sam was. Meg looked at him, her
eyes full of love. She so badly wanted to say those
three little words. *I love you.*

Meg mustered up her courage. "Luke," she
began, but stopped suddenly. *Just say it,* she told
herself. Luke couldn't help but notice the way she
was looking at him.

"What?" Luke asked, his eyes darting around uncomfortably.

"I—I . . . ," Meg stammered, trying to spit the words out. "I only have fifteen more minutes," she said, chickening out.

Luke considered that. "Fifteen minutes?" He looked around the store. It was still empty. He smiled. "A lot can be done in fifteen minutes."

Meg raised her eyebrows suspiciously. "What'd you have in mind?" she asked, flirting a little.

Luke grabbed her hand and led her to Mr. Greenwood's office. Quickly he closed the door and started pulling the blinds down over the large glass window that looked out on the entire store. Meg laughed to herself, remembering the last time she and Luke had made out in Mr. Greenwood's office. It was a complete and utter disaster. Mostly because they never actually made out. Instead Meg just made a fool out of herself.

A few months earlier Patty had walked in on Meg and Luke kissing up in her attic on her bed, and as bad luck and bad timing would have it, Patty burst through the door at the exact moment Luke was unhooking Meg's bra. Patty, who'd taken to reading trashy romance novels, used her powers of observation to hypothesize that Luke's smooth technique could mean only one thing: This wasn't Luke's first time going to second. Patty's annoying—and surprisingly accurate—observations threatened Meg to the point that Meg needed a conclusive answer. She needed to know how much experience Luke really had.

In questioning Luke about his past she realized that she wasn't his first—or even his second. Secretly Meg was horrified. Aside from one disastrous date and one staged kiss with Jimmy Riley under the mistletoe on *Bandstand,* Luke was Meg's first and only boyfriend. When it came to experience, Meg had just rounded first, was anxious to approach second, and had absolutely no intention of going to home plate anytime in the near future. Confused, Meg turned to Roxanne for advice.

"Be spontaneous," Roxanne instructed. "Alluring. Devil-may-care."

Meg looked at Roxanne blankly. "I can't even pretend to imagine what you mean," she admitted.

"Show him that you're more experienced than he thinks you are," Roxanne said, describing how Meg could surprise Luke at work, drag him into Mr. Greenwood's office, and, well, seduce him.

Meg stared at Roxanne in disbelief. "This is Luke

we're talking about!" she said, emphasizing that there was no way that was going to happen.

Roxanne shrugged. "Fine, Meg. Keep going at a snail's pace," she said to her hopelessly unspontaneous friend. "And kiss your first second good-bye." Meg rolled her eyes, but inside she was afraid Roxanne was right.

Later that day, after *Bandstand,* Meg took Roxanne's words to heart, pulling Luke into Mr. Greenwood's office and kissing him, trying her best to be spontaneous, alluring, and devil-may-care. But instead of spontaneous, her actions felt forced. Instead of alluring, she felt silly. And instead of devil-may-care, she realized she *did* care. After Luke pushed her away, she realized that she had completely humiliated herself.

But now, standing with Luke in Mr. Greenwood's office once again, she knew that their relationship was different. Nine months of dating Luke meant Meg had a little more experience with boys, and during that time she had found out that Luke had a little less experience with girls than it had originally seemed. It turned out one of his seconds was a fluke—at summer camp he tripped and a girl's chest simply broke his fall. Meg had laughed at the fact that he was so insecure about his own inexperience that he would count such a blatant accident. But that's what endeared Luke to her as well. She looked at him as he finished pulling the blinds down and turned around. Within an instant they were kissing.

Meg felt her stomach flip with excitement, happy to be in Luke's arms. Despite their constant bickering and arguing about everything from Meg's love of *Bandstand* to Luke's bizarre hatred of Philly cheesesteaks, they were attracted to each other and had been spending a majority of the summer making out during drive-in movies.

Luke pulled her closer, unbuttoning her sweater as they kissed. Slowly his hands reached around her body and moved down her back, untucking her blouse. A few months ago this would have sent Meg running to Roxanne with a handful of questions, but after an entire summer with Luke this wasn't anything new. Meg felt the clasp on her bra loosen and unhook as Luke slid his hand around her body.

Suddenly the door flung open!

"Who do I have to kiss to get some service around here?" Roxanne joked, fully aware of the moment she was interrupting.

"Roxanne!" Meg gasped, struggling to rehook her bra, her face bright red with embarrassment.

Roxanne took in the scene, impressed. "Wow . . . ,"

she commented. "You two seem to be taking things to the next—"

"Don't you have something to be doing, Roxanne?" Luke interrupted, as politely as possible.

"Yeah. Hanging out with my best friend on her birthday," Roxanne quipped. Luke threw an annoyed glance in Meg's direction. Unfortunately, dating Meg meant more Roxanne in his life than he quite knew what to do with. Chronically single yet perpetually lip-locked with someone, Roxanne had perfected the art of being the third wheel and play-by-play commentator whenever he and Meg spent time together.

Meg quickly finished buttoning up her sweater.

"You'd better be careful," Roxanne warned. "If your mom saw this, she wouldn't let you out of the house either."

Meg suddenly looked at her watch, realizing. "I only have ten more minutes until my mom comes."

Roxanne nudged Luke, who reached into the desk drawer, pulling out an envelope. "So," Roxanne began. "Meg." Meg smiled, excited for whatever Roxanne and Luke had in store for her. "I've known you since we were six years old. . . ."

"And I've known you since you were fifteen," Luke added, not wanting to be left out.

"We've been through everything together," Roxanne said. "We've been through good times—"

"And bad," Luke reminded her. "Like that fight you just had?" Roxanne shot Luke the evil eye. Meg and Roxanne had just recently made up from a summer-long fight that began over Meg's friendship with Carol, a popular senior from East Catholic who had taken an instant liking to Meg and an instant dislike to Roxanne, creating a major problem between the two best friends. Now, however, Roxanne chose to ignore Luke's comment and continued with her thoughtful birthday speech.

Roxanne continued reminiscing. "Dancing on *Bandstand,* becoming regulars, signing autographs for our fans . . ."

"You know, all the important things in life," Luke commented sarcastically.

Roxanne couldn't take it anymore. Unable to hide how annoyed she was at Luke's incessant barbs about *Bandstand,* she exclaimed to Luke, "You're being a real jerk right now!"

"Roxanne—," Meg tried to interject.

"What? He is!" Roxanne said, pointing a finger at Luke. "Even on your birthday he has to make fun of *Bandstand!*"

Luke defended himself. "I'm not—"

Roxanne put her hand over his mouth as she turned to face Meg. "Don't you get sick of it?" she asked. "His stupid little glasses, his challenged fashion sense, his holier-than-thou comments on all things un-*Bandstand*?" Meg looked at Luke, who mumbled something muffled and indistinguishable from under Roxanne's hand.

"What?" Roxanne said, annoyed. Luke again mumbled something. "I'm sorry," Roxanne taunted. "I can't understand you."

"Roxanne!" Meg said, pulling Roxanne's hand away from Luke's mouth.

"I said, five minutes," Luke answered, frustrated. "And keep your hands away from my face. Who knows where they've been." Roxanne opened her mouth to protest.

"Stop it! Both of you!" Meg demanded. "I only have"—she looked at her watch—"four minutes and thirty-seven seconds until I'm trapped in my house until school starts again!"

"Hopefully this will change that," Roxanne offered. She nudged Luke and indicated the white envelope. Luke grabbed it off the desk and handed it to Meg.

"Happy birthday, Meg," Luke said sincerely.

"What is it?" she wondered aloud, taking the envelope.

"Well, open it, silly," Roxanne encouraged. Meg ripped open the envelope, pulled out its contents, and screamed with joy.

"Oh my gosh!" Meg cried. "Is this a joke?" Luke and Roxanne looked at each other, their bickering already forgotten as it was replaced by the joy of seeing Meg so stunned and surprised.

"Seriously?" Meg said, knowing this couldn't possibly be her gift. It was too impressive. "I don't get it. What does this mean?"

"It means," Roxanne said, smiling, "that we're taking you to see the Beatles."

"Beatles tickets!" Meg yelled excitedly. "We're going to see the Beatles!" Meg jumped on Luke and tried to hug Roxanne simultaneously. Playfully Roxanne jumped on Luke as well, and he toppled backward onto Mr. Greenwood's desk.

After a minute, when they all were upright and composed, Meg asked, "How on earth did you get these? I thought the show was sold out." She looked at Roxanne. "You and I waited in line for hours. It was completely sold out."

"That was the *Philly* show," Luke corrected. "But read the ticket."

Meg looked again, more closely this time. "'Atlantic City,'" she read. "The show's in Atlantic City?"

"And there's one ticket for each of us," Roxanne pointed out. "So you wouldn't have to choose who to bring. Not that it would have been that difficult of a choice," she added knowingly.

"I can't believe you got us these tickets, Roxanne," Meg said.

"Well, actually . . ." Roxanne looked at Luke.

Luke shrugged, downplaying the effort he had made. "Mr. Greenwood had a connection." What he didn't mention was that he'd be washing Mr. Greenwood's car every Saturday for the next year as payback for the favor.

Meg threw her arms around Luke's neck and kissed him. "I have the best boyfriend ever," she declared.

"Hey, what am I?" Roxanne asked defensively. "Chopped liver?"

"No," Luke reminded her, "you're the one in charge of transportation."

"What?" Roxanne said, looking confused. Covering, she added, "Oh, right. Transportation." After a moment Roxanne turned to Meg. "When are you getting your driver's license again?"

Meg did a double take. Surely Roxanne wasn't implying that *Meg* would drive. "And," added Roxanne, "what are the chances of borrowing your dad's car?"

Meg was momentarily distracted by the fact that Roxanne's question reminded her she had her driver's test the following day, but the mention of her dad brought Meg crashing back to reality. Who was she kidding? The idea of her dad letting her out of the house was unlikely, let alone borrowing his car to go to a Beatles concert in New Jersey with Luke and Roxanne. Meg's heart sank.

"I can't take these tickets," Meg said sadly, her spirit deflated like a giant balloon. "My dad . . . he's never gonna let me . . ." She trailed off in disbelief that she was handing back Beatles tickets. Her one chance to see John, George, Ringo, and Paul— *especially* Paul.

Meg remembered the day back in February when the Beatles "landed" in America. It was officially Beatlemania. If it weren't for Dick Clark declaring it Beatles Day on *American Bandstand* and playing "I Want to Hold Your Hand," the kids on *Bandstand* would never have allowed Michael Brooks to tear them away from the television sets and force them into the bleachers so that he could start the countdown to begin the show. At the time all the kids figured, if they couldn't watch the Beatles live, dancing to their music was a close second.

"Meg," Roxanne said, snapping her out of her Beatles reverie. "You're sixteen now. You're practically an adult. It's time to take control of your life, your future, your—"

"Mom's here," Luke interrupted, gesturing toward the front door. Meg and Roxanne spun around and saw Helen standing in the doorway, hands on her hips. Panicked, Meg looked at her watch, which confirmed her worst fears. She was late.

Five

Meg and Helen pulled into the garage, surprised to see the Pryor's TV and Radio truck in the driveway, which meant one thing: Jack was home. Meg cringed, knowing that now, after being late, it was unlikely her mom would stick up for her. Was it possible to be double grounded?

"Mom, I'm . . ." Before Meg could finish explaining, Helen was out of the car and heading into the house. Meg hurried after her, knowing that her mom was mad. She feared that if her mom said anything to her dad, her already slim chances of going to the Beatles concert would be completely obliterated.

As Meg followed Helen into the house she noticed her dad sitting in the den watching a ball game on TV. He turned his head as they entered and looked directly at Meg.

"Where've you been?" he asked her pointedly, already expecting that he wasn't going to like any excuse Meg could conjure up.

As Meg opened her mouth to explain Helen

interrupted. "Driving," Helen said. "We were practicing." Meg, a mixture of shock and gratitude etched on her face, threw a quick sidelong glance at her mom.

"My driver's test is tomorrow," Meg reminded Jack. "At ten."

Jack stood up and turned off the TV. "When's dinner?" he asked Helen.

"Half an hour," she said as she unpacked the extra groceries she'd just picked up from the market. Jack looked at his watch. He grabbed the keys off the counter.

"You got plans right now?" Jack asked, more into thin air than to anybody directly.

Meg looked around, confused. "Me?" she said. Her dad knew full well she had no plans. At least not any plans that he was privy to.

"Yeah, you," he answered. "Let's go."

"Where?" Meg asked.

"Practice makes perfect," Jack responded. Meg looked at her mom in disbelief. Meg had been begging her dad to take her driving for weeks. Helen looked up from her cutting board, where she was chopping vegetables for a salad, and smiled.

"Meg," Jack warned for the third time. "Leave the radio alone." So far they'd been driving for fifteen minutes, and Meg had fixed her hair in the rearview mirror, noticed a cute boy walking down the sidewalk, and changed the radio station three times in search of a song she liked.

"But Dad," she complained. "Good music helps me drive."

"Not as much as keeping your hands on the wheel," he said. "Meg, ten and two. Remember? Ten and two." Meg shifted her hands to the correct placement. She approached a stop sign and gradually slowed down until she came to a complete stop.

"Good, Meg," Jack encouraged. "Now, step on the—"

Meg hit the gas pedal too hard and they went flying out into the intersection. Scared, she slammed on the brake pedal. The car lurched to an instant stop.

"Meg!" Jack yelled, feeling especially vulnerable in the passenger seat.

"Don't yell at me!" Meg cried.

Jack tried to calm himself down. "Just . . . just . . . ," he stammered, trying to find the words. "Just pull over."

Meg tried to compose herself. Her dad said, "Turn signal, Meg. Use your turn signal." The windshield wipers went on. "No. Your turn signal," Jack reiterated, now practically yelling again. Meg was getting increasingly freaked out as a line of cars formed behind her. She managed to pull over to the curb.

One guy yelled out his window, "Learn how to drive, lady!"

"I'm trying," Meg screamed back, getting dangerously close to nervous-breakdown territory.

"All right, calm down," Jack instructed. She leaned against the driver's side window, her head resting in her hand. "The point, Meg," Jack said, beginning to lecture her, "isn't to confuse the other drivers around you. The point is to clearly and effectively—"

Suddenly she couldn't take it—his voice, the lecturing, all the events of the past twenty-four hours. The floodgates opened. Tears poured out of her eyes, and her was body racked with sobs.

Jack didn't know what to make of this. "Meg, it's okay," he said hesitantly, trying to calm his teenage daughter. "Turn signal, windshield wipers . . . easy mistake. You'll get it."

Meg shook her head. It wasn't that. Her tears were about something more. Jack realized that as clear as he'd been in punishing her, he hadn't been clear enough in telling her how worried he'd been about her, how happy he was to find out she was safe at home, and just how much he truly loved her. Now, with being grounded on her sixteenth birthday, with not being able to spend the day with her friends, with the pressure of her driver's test looming on the horizon, it all seemed like too much for Meg to handle.

"Don't worry about the test," he said, attempting to comfort Meg. "Look at the way your uncle Pete drives . . . and he passed." Jack's attempt to make her feel better wasn't working. If anything, the mention of Pete made her cry even harder than before. "Meg?" he finally asked, realizing that her tears were about more than parallel parking and three-point turns. "What's wrong? Is this about getting your license?"

Meg shook her head. "Have you . . . heard . . ." Meg choked out the words between sobs. "Have you heard from Henry?"

"What?" Jack asked, surprised, wondering how Henry could be a source of her tears.

"Henry," Meg repeated. "Did you talk to him today?"

Jack nodded, suddenly realizing what this was about. It had nothing to do with Henry. He should have known that after the riot there would be only one person on Meg's mind. Sam Walker.

"Sam's fine," Jack said.

"You know that?" Meg asked, her sobs becoming less frequent. "He made it home? From the riot?"

Jack's face clearly said that he didn't want to talk about the riot or Sam. But to appease her, he answered, "I spoke to Henry. And Sam's fine."

Meg breathed a huge sigh of relief. Finally it was over. It felt as if a monstrous weight had just been lifted off her shoulders. Jack sat, searching for what to say. About Sam. About the riot. About her birthday.

"Meg," Jack began. "Yesterday, knowing you were out there . . . caught in that mess . . ." He thought for a moment, unsure of exactly what he was trying to say. "I know I'm hard on you sometimes. And I know you don't always understand why. We both have tempers, you know? We're stubborn." Meg wiped away her tears and nodded, acknowledging that it was true. Sometimes, she realized, she was more like her father than she cared to admit. "And I know when I got home last night . . . well, we were both pretty upset . . . about everything. . . ." He trailed off. He wanted to tell her how he felt, but it was hard to find the right words.

When he'd realized Meg was out there, at the Girard store, he'd felt as if he'd been punched in the gut a thousand times in a row. The fear that something might happen to his daughter was numbing. He and Henry ran out of the main store, trying to get through police barriers, desperate to reach their children. Then they arrived at the Girard store in time to find . . . nothing. The kids were missing, and the building was burning down.

Jack looked at his daughter, sixteen years old, more a woman than a child. Now that she was a teenager, he had to strain to remember the little girl who used to hang on his leg when he walked, and would worm her way onto his lap while he was reading the paper. He used to marvel at the energy Meg and Roxanne had as they tore around the house and yard, trying to hide from Patty. He laughed to himself, remembering a silly game Roxanne and Meg had convinced Patty to play, called "don't let each other see each other." They told her that every time she saw them, she had to scream and run in the opposite direction. It kept Patty out of their hair for a week, until she caught on to their plan. He looked at his daughter, taking in how grown-up she suddenly seemed.

"Dad?" Meg reminded him. "You were saying something?"

Jack tried again, choosing his words carefully. "About yesterday. I know you were . . . I mean . . . your heart was in the right place. And now today's your birthday. . . ." Jack couldn't figure out why it was so hard for him to apologize. Not that he'd been wrong for yelling at her—she deserved that. But with it being her birthday and all, a part of him wanted to give her a break, to tell her that he'd overreacted, to tell her . . .

"I'm proud of you, Meg," he said quietly. "I don't say that enough. But I am." Surprised by her dad's outpouring of emotion, Meg realized now might be her chance. "Happy birthday, Meg," Jack said. Meg basked in the glow of her father's approval for a minute, until he said, "Okay, let's put the car in drive."

Feeling more confident, Meg pulled back out onto the tree-lined street. As they drove around for another fifteen minutes Meg wondered if now was the time to mention the Beatles concert. Things seemed to be going well between her father and her. Meg had even successfully parallel-parked twice and had filled the car up with gas.

"So, Luke and Roxanne did something really special for my birthday," she mentioned, gently feeling out the situation.

"Uh-huh," Jack said, focusing more on her driving than on the words she was saying. "Meg, the light," he reminded her.

"What?" Meg asked.

"It's red."

Meg looked up and slammed on the brakes. When the light turned green, Meg tried again.

"They got me tickets to a show," Meg explained.

"A show?" Jack asked. "Take a right on Chestnut," he added.

"Yeah, but not just for any show," Meg said, summoning her courage. "To see the Beatles."

"The Beatles?" Jack said, impressed. "Quite a gift."

"Luke's boss, Mr. Greenwood, had a connection," Meg explained. "In Atlantic City."

"What's Atlantic City got to do with anything?" Jack asked. "Left on Oak."

Meg tried to sound as casual as possible. "That's where the concert is."

"They'll have a good time," Jack said. "Luke and Roxanne."

Meg wasn't sure what he meant by that. "Yeah, I think it'll be really fun," she said. "*We'll* have a really good time." She took a left onto Oak.

"Who? You?" Jack asked incredulously. Meg's

heart started to beat faster, and she knew before he opened his mouth that the next sentence Jack spoke would be, "You're not going to Atlantic City, Meg."

Meg turned to look at Jack. "But Dad—"

"Eyes on the road!" Jack yelled.

Meg tried to refocus on the road but was distracted by the prospect of missing the Beatles. "Luke worked really hard to get those tickets," she complained. "If I don't go—"

"Not *if*," Jack corrected her. "You're not going."

"It's not fair!" she protested, her eyes welling up with tears.

"Meg, I don't wanna hear it," Jack said adamantly. "Don't miss the house."

Meg quickly cranked the wheel to the right, tearing into the driveway, and before Jack could warn her, she sideswiped the mailbox.

Six

The next morning when the alarm went off at exactly 8:05 A.M., Meg couldn't remember why she'd set it or where she needed to be. She bolted upright at the sudden ringing sound in her ears and shut the alarm off quickly. With summer almost over she hadn't set an alarm in months. Flopping back down and pulling the covers over her head, she decided she'd rather stay in bed than face another day without her friends, without *Bandstand,* without any freedom whatsoever. With nothing to wake up for, she let herself drift back to sleep.

As she dozed in and out of consciousness she thought about how angry she was with her dad: the way he'd grounded her, the way he'd lectured her about parallel parking and three-point turns, the way he'd yelled after she hit the mailbox. And suddenly she remembered why her alarm was set— she was taking her driver's test today! If by some miracle she passed, she'd have more freedom than she knew what to do with. Realizing she was going to be late, she kicked off the covers, grabbed her bathrobe, and ran for the shower. As Meg walked down the hallway to the bathroom Patty seized the opportunity to sneak around her, running into the bathroom and slamming the door in Meg's face.

"Patty!" Meg yelled, pounding on the door. "It's my turn!" Meg heard the knobs of the bathtub turning and water pouring out. Meg pounded on the door even harder.

After a moment Patty threw open the door. "Yes, Margaret?" she asked as sweetly as possible.

Meg tried to push the door open, but Patty stopped it with her foot. Patty was awfully strong for a twelve-year-old. "Get out, Patty," Meg said through clenched teeth.

"I'll be happy to get out," Patty said, smiling, "when I'm done with my bath."

Meg bristled, knowing full well that Patty was simply doing whatever would take the absolute longest. "You don't even take baths," she said. "Will takes baths!" She threw herself against the door. It flew open so fast and with such force that the doorknob hit the wall behind it, making an obvious dent in the plaster. Meg cringed.

"The mailbox wasn't enough?" Patty asked. "Now you have to destroy the bathroom, too?"

"Shut up, Patty!" Meg said, her frustration bubbling over.

"Mom!" Patty yelled. "Meg told me to shut up!"

"Meg! Get down here!" Helen shouted from downstairs.

"But Mom . . . ," Meg protested, glaring at Patty.

"Now!" Helen yelled back.

Patty raised her eyebrows, feeling very satisfied with herself. "You'd better hurry," she sneered. "You wouldn't want to be late to *fail* your driver's test."

Meg's eyes narrowed. "When I do get my license," she assured her sister, "I'm not driving you anywhere. Ever."

"Meg!" Helen called angrily. "Now!"

With no time to shower or to eat breakfast, Meg was a bundle of stress and nervous energy as she pulled into the driveway of the Department of Motor Vehicles for her driver's test. JJ, who sat in the passenger seat secretly gripping the armrest in fear, had offered to accompany Meg to the test, since both their parents were in different phases of being angry with her. Jack was still upset with her for the mailbox incident, not to mention for going to North Philly alone, and Helen had threatened to ground Meg if she told Patty to shut up one more time.

"I already *am* grounded," Meg had reminded her mother, which seemed to upset Helen even more. That's when JJ had stepped in and offered to take her instead.

Meg put the car in park and shut it off. She looked at her watch. It was ten o'clock sharp. She was right on time.

"Good luck, Meg," JJ said. "And remember, when you're driving, leave the radio off."

"You sound like Dad," Meg admonished.

"That was a low blow," JJ responded as he laced his shoes tighter. "I'm going for a run," JJ told her. "Be back in an hour."

"You're not coming in with me?" Meg asked, her nerves starting to show.

"Come on, Meg," JJ said. "You're sixteen now. You want freedom. You earn it yourself." Meg wasn't sure whether he was being harsh or supportive.

He patted her on the shoulder. "Meg," he said kindly. "I know you can do it." As JJ took off running down the street Meg took a deep breath and went into the ominous brick building, hoping that this time JJ was right.

Inside, while the building crawled with anxious sixteen-year-olds and their supportive parents, Meg struggled with the written portion of the driver's test. Despite the fact that she and Sam had spent the entire summer quizzing each other for the written exam, all the answers seemed to evaporate into thin air now that she needed to know them. Even the easier questions, about things like driving in fog, blind spots, and parking on an incline, were making her second-guess herself. When she finished, she wrung her hands nervously, convinced she had failed—until a man in a coat and tie, holding a clipboard, came out to the waiting area.

"Meg Pryor?" he called out, glancing around.

Meg looked up quickly. She was so nervous she'd nearly chewed her fingernails off. "I'm Meg Pryor," she responded, standing up and smoothing down her pleated skirt, wondering if the news was good or bad.

"Congratulations, young lady," the man said. As Meg smiled broadly her heart skipped a beat. Had she really passed?

"Come with me," he added. Meg's happiness quickly faded when she remembered she still had the clutch-popping, brake-slamming, mailbox-hitting portion of her test left. She fished in her purse for her keys and slowly followed the instructor out to her car. Luckily, since her parents had a car, she didn't have to drive one of the cars provided by the DMV. She could drive something familiar, something with the mirrors and seat already adjusted to her liking, something where the radio was already set to her favorite station.

As she opened the car door she looked back toward the building. A boy was walking inside. At the sight of him Meg did a double take. Although she could see only his back, she knew without a doubt that the boy was Sam. She was sure of it. Meg was about to yell his name, when the instructor spoke.

"Miss?" he said. "You're driving."

"What?" Meg responded, distracted by the sight of the door shutting behind Sam and frustrated that she couldn't run after him.

"You're driving," the man reiterated. Meg realized she was at the passenger door.

"Oh, I'm sorry," Meg said, flustered. She walked around the car, hurriedly slipped into the driver's seat, and started the ignition. When the car lurched backward, she reasoned that the instructor knew as well as she did that they were in for a bumpy ride.

In retrospect she couldn't really say the driving portion of the exam went well. The instructor grabbed the wheel twice as she was parallel-parking, her three-point turn was more like a six-point turn, and she was so anxious to get back to the DMV to see Sam she ended up being reprimanded for speeding. Twice. By the time she pulled back into the space at the DMV, she was sure she'd failed. The instructor stared at his clipboard, making checks and Xs with his red pen.

After an agonizing wait Meg couldn't take it anymore. Mustering up all of her courage, she finally asked, "Did I pass?" She waited for what felt like an eternity for him to answer.

But instead of giving her the results, he asked a question that caught her completely off guard. "You're on that show, right?" the instructor asked. "*American Bandstand*?" Meg nodded nervously, wondering what *Bandstand* had to do with her driving abilities. "My daughter loves that show," he continued. "You and Jimmy were her favorite couple."

"Really?" Meg said. Sometimes she forgot how popular she and Jimmy Riley were. They'd been hounded for autographs and even been mobbed at a record signing at the Vinyl Crocodile. The teen magazines made them sound like the perfect couple.

"Really," he answered. "She's been waiting outside

in line with her best friend all summer long." Meg smiled, remembering that she and Roxanne used to do that every day before they became regulars. Even the rain and snow couldn't keep them away from waiting in that line, hoping to be chosen.

Suddenly Meg realized that her semicelebrity status could be used to her advantage. Roxanne would have been so proud. "What's her name?" Meg asked. "Your daughter?"

"Natalie," he responded. "Natalie Scott."

"Will she be there today?" Meg asked, hoping it wasn't bribery. And if it was, she hoped that wasn't against the law. "She waits outside WFIL?"

"Every day. Like clockwork," he said. "My wife took her the last two days because of everything that's been going on. You hear about that riot?"

Meg nodded politely as her stomach lurched at the flashback of Sam's face as she drove off, leaving him behind. She was anxious to go inside and find him. But Mr. Scott went right on talking. It seemed *Bandstand* was more on his radar than the Philadelphia riot.

"She's there with her best friend," he continued. "Thought today might be their lucky day."

"Maybe it is," Meg said, smiling. "I'll talk to the line guy. Get them on."

"Really? You can do that?" the instructor asked, sounding somewhat amazed. If it meant she was any closer to getting her driver's license, Meg would do anything. "It's that easy?"

As she nodded happily Meg felt like a real celebrity. Feeling as though she had buttered up the instructor sufficiently, she couldn't wait any longer for the results of her driver's test.

"So," Meg said nervously. "Did I pass?"

Mr. Scott smiled and handed her a piece of paper. "Here you go," he said.

Meg searched the paper for her score and looked up happily. "You're serious?" she asked, thrilled. "I passed? Just like that?"

"It's that easy," he said, smiling. "Congratulations, Miss Pryor. You passed." Meg clutched the piece of paper tightly, knowing that from here on out her life would be different.

After thanking Mr. Scott profusely, Meg ran inside in search of Sam. She found him in the waiting room, where he'd just completed his written test.

"Sam!" Meg yelled, running over to him. He stood up at the sight of her.

"Meg," he said softly. Meg wanted to tell him everything—how she had tried to call, how she had hung up when Henry answered, how her dad had grounded her, how terrible she had felt leaving him alone in the riot. She stopped right in front of him, not knowing quite what to do. Her instinct was to hug him, but she suddenly realized that she'd never hugged Sam before. She stepped forward with her arms outstretched, when Anita appeared.

Anita was strikingly beautiful, with flawless skin, perfect posture, and big brown eyes. "Hi," she said, not quite sure what to make of Meg and Sam. Meg knew Anita from the blues concert and the Valentine's Day dance at East Catholic, but the girls didn't know each other well. Anita grabbed hold of Sam's hand.

"Hi," Meg responded shyly, stepping away from Sam. She felt as if she'd just done something wrong. There was so much Meg wanted to ask Sam, but with Anita standing next to him, holding his hand, she couldn't help but feel awkward, although she wasn't quite sure why.

"Did you pass?" Sam asked, gesturing to the paper she was holding.

"Yeah," Meg said happily. "You?"

"Just took the written," he answered.

"What'd you get?" asked Meg.

"A perfect score," Anita responded proudly. Sam blushed.

"You're kidding!" Meg said, incredulous. "I got four wrong, including—"

"Let me guess . . . ," Sam began.

"The railroad track question," they said simultaneously. Meg laughed. For a moment everything felt normal again, as if nothing had changed, as if things were as they'd always been. But the feeling was fleeting as Anita put a damper on their high spirits.

"Meg," Anita said. "I'm sorry to hear about what happened to your dad's store in the riot."

"Thanks," Meg said shyly. "It's really sad. For both our dads." Sam nodded. His own father truly shared in the loss.

"Was your friend okay?" Meg asked tentatively. "Willy . . . was he . . . ."

Sam shook his head, correcting her. "Willy Johnson's not my friend."

Admonished, Meg felt her face redden. "I know . . . I just thought . . . ," she stammered self-consciously, feeling as if she was talking about things she didn't quite understand.

"He's in the hospital," Sam told her gently. "The bullet—it went through to his spine. The doctors, they don't know if he's gonna make it."

"And Nathan?" Meg asked softly, hoping Sam's

cousin was okay. Last time she had seen Nathan, the police were taking him away.

"Nathan's in jail," Sam admitted. Meg shook her head in disbelief. It all seemed so strange—the city burning down, someone shot and paralyzed, someone else in jail.

"I'm so—," Meg began, but before she could tell Sam just how sorry she was, his name was called.

"Sam Walker?" an instructor read off his clipboard. Sam spun around at the sound of his name. "You ready, Mr. Walker?"

"I'd better go," Sam said to Meg. "Congratulations."

"You too," Meg said. "I mean, good luck. Not that you need it," she added nervously. Waving good-bye to both Sam and Anita, she walked over to line up to get her picture taken. As she watched Sam walk outside with the instructor she felt as though Anita was looking at her, her gaze burning into the back of Meg's head. Meg didn't dare turn around to check. When it was Meg's turn in front of the camera, a middle-aged woman instructed her to smile. Meg forced one as the camera snapped her picture.

"It looks . . . fine," Roxanne said, inspecting Meg's new driver's license. They were running from the bus stop to WFIL, knowing they were going to be late for *Bandstand*.

Of course, Meg wasn't supposed to be at *Bandstand* at all. But with her dad at the Girard store all day, trying to salvage anything he could, she knew he wouldn't see her on TV. And her mom had taken Patty and Will to the community pool for the day. As long as she could beat them home, no one would be the wiser. Plus, she had no choice—she'd guaranteed Mr. Scott she'd get his daughter in. Today. If Meg went back on her word, she figured that the DMV might revoke her license.

Meg and Roxanne rushed past the smaller-than-usual line forming outside the entrance to the studio. Roxanne continued to inspect Meg's less-than-flattering driver's license picture.

"Fine means bad," Meg responded, snatching the laminated card out of Roxanne's clutches. "Thanks a lot." They stopped at the side door under the marquee.

"So it's not your best picture," Roxanne consoled her. "It's not like anyone's going to see it." They stopped and waited for the line guy to let them through.

"How'd you do?" the line guy asked Meg. "You get it? Your license?"

"Yeah," Meg exclaimed happily.

"Let's see the picture," he said. Meg tried to ignore him and started to rush inside, until she remembered her promise to Mr. Scott.

"Is there anybody named Natalie Scott here?" Meg asked loudly to the kids waiting in line. A mother nudged her teenage daughter, and an auburn-haired, petite girl shot her hand up in the air.

"I'm Natalie," she said, waving, her brown eyes full of hope.

Meg gestured for her to come to the front of the line. "Come here," Meg said. "And bring your friend."

Natalie grabbed the hand of an identical-looking doe-eyed teenager and dragged her to the front of the line. Meg introduced herself. "I'm Meg, and this is my friend Roxanne."

Roxanne smiled politely. "Hi there," she said, casually flaunting her nonchalant celebrity attitude.

"You both are my favorite dancers on the show," Natalie gushed as her friend nodded furiously in agreement. She turned to Meg. "When you and Jimmy kissed under the mistletoe, I just about died." Meg remembered that she had too.

As the line guy opened the door to let more fans in Meg heard the familiar sound of "Bandstand Boogie" opening the show. "How would you girls like to be on *American Bandstand* today?" Meg asked, knowing she was about to make their entire year. Natalie and her friend looked at each other just as Meg and Roxanne had done almost a year ago when they found out they would be on *American Bandstand*. The girls hugged each other and screamed.

When *Bandstand* ended, Meg and Roxanne took Natalie and her friend, whose name was Kate, on a tour of WFIL and got them autographs from Dick Clark and many of the regulars. Then Meg and Roxanne made a beeline for the door—but Michael Brooks stopped them.

"Girls, you got a second?" Michael asked quickly. Meg didn't have a lot of time if she was going to beat both her parents home. She huddled with the other regulars for Michael's announcement.

"Now that you're all here," he said, "I need your help with something." The dancers murmured curiously to one another, wondering what was going on.

"Anything," Roxanne said with a smile, raising her eyebrows. She'd had a crush on Michael Brooks for ages.

"It's very last minute, but I need you all to be in attendance," he explained.

"Where?" Meg asked.

"Wildwood Pier," Michael answered. "In three days." Wildwood was a town along the Jersey Shore where Meg and her family vacationed every summer. "Mr. Clark had the idea to do another hop," explained Michael.

"Not that I have any problem going to the beach again," Roxanne said, "but didn't we just do that?"

All the regulars had gone down to the shore just a few weeks earlier to dance to live music with lucky vacationers on the pier. But Michael explained that since the riot, not only had attendance on *Bandstand* been low—understandably—but even worse, musical acts were hesitant about coming to Philly. Performers were backing out left and right. The network needed a new location to entice both performers and fans back to the show. The hop had been a huge success earlier in the summer, so it seemed like an easy solution to what was becoming a serious problem.

"I know this is short notice," Michael explained. "So if you can't come, it's okay. But please try. You're the people who make this show special."

As Michael continued to go over the details Roxanne squeezed Meg's arm excitedly. "Three days from now is the Beatles show, Meg. It's perfect," she whispered happily. "We dance down at the shore and swing by Atlantic City on our way home." Incredulous, Meg looked at Roxanne.

"My dad will never let me—," Meg began.

Roxanne interrupted. "What your dad doesn't know won't hurt him," she assured Meg.

"I know it won't hurt him, Rox," Meg said. "But when he finds out, he might hurt *me*."

Roxanne looked at her best friend. "*If* he finds out."

"Roxanne," Meg said, "with my dad it's not a matter of *if*, it's a matter of *when*."

"Meg," Roxanne said knowingly. "Three words: Make it happen." She interlaced her arm with Meg's and dragged her toward the door. "Because if you don't, I will."

Seven

Two days later, with the Beatles show only a day away, Meg still hadn't mustered up the courage to mention the hop to her father. She was afraid all hopes of sneaking off to the Beatles concert afterward would be dashed the moment he said no. She sat on her bed, watching as Roxanne debated between two nail polish colors, Razzle Red and Petal Pink.

"You've got to do it, Meg," Roxanne urged, choosing the red one and shaking the bottle before she opened it. "If not for yourself, do it for Paul and Ringo. They need our support."

Meg sifted through her 45s, looking for a Beatles record, knowing her only opportunity to hear them might be on the record player in her attic. "Roxanne," she said, "he's said no to everything else. The hop isn't gonna be any different." Meg knew there was no more arguing with her dad. She'd tried to communicate that to Roxanne, but Roxanne wasn't giving up without a fight. As much as Jack's answer was *always* no, Roxanne never took no for an answer.

"He can't say no to the hop. It's your responsibility, your obligation to the show," Roxanne reminded her as she unscrewed the nail polish cap. "Besides, if you don't show up, Michael will kick you off." Meg spun around, shocked.

"Michael said that?" Meg asked, momentarily panicked. Would she really be kicked off *Bandstand* if she didn't go to Wildwood?

"Well . . . no," Roxanne confessed. "But your dad doesn't need to know that." Meg breathed a sigh of relief. *Thank God,* she thought. *Bandstand* was the best part of her life. Without it, her life would be boring, empty, and disturbingly average.

But her only other option was lying. Not only was she horribly bad at it, she hated doing it. It made her feel so guilty she felt like the lies were eating at her insides as punishment.

Suddenly Roxanne lit up. "I've got it!" She claimed she had a foolproof plan. Another lie, Meg assumed. She never ceased to be amazed by the ease with which Roxanne lied, though Meg supposed it was easier when you were lying to someone else's parents.

"Tell him if you get kicked off *Bandstand,* you could turn to a life of crime."

•

"What?" Meg laughed. She couldn't wait to hear Roxanne's shaky logic for this one. Not to mention that the number of lies Meg was supposed to tell—getting kicked off the show *and* entering a life of crime—had suddenly doubled.

"If you didn't have *Bandstand* after school," Roxanne explained, "you'd have all this free time to do other things. *Bad* things."

"What bad things?" Meg asked, trying not to laugh.

"Well, for one, you'd have more time to make out with Luke. Which means you'd be moving much faster than you already are. And from what I saw the other day, you pretty much had second base covered." Meg blushed, embarrassed. "Which means that with a little more alone time, by next week Luke could be rounding third; by the time school starts, he'll be sliding into—"

"Roxanne!" Meg gasped, interrupting.

"And it's not just Luke," Roxanne added. "You'd have time to do *other* things—bad, bad things. Like shoplift, get in fights, rob banks . . ."

"Rob banks?" Meg asked, incredulous. "Roxanne, I'm not robbing a bank!"

"You know what I mean," Roxanne said. But Meg didn't know. As far as she was concerned, Roxanne was grasping at straws.

"That excuse is crazy!" Meg said. "It's never going to work."

"Fine," Roxanne said, undeterred. "How about this?" She thought for a moment and finished painting the toenails on her right foot. Meg waited in anticipation of what Roxanne would come up with.

"Roxanne, what's taking so long?" Meg warned, joking. "I just turned seventeen waiting for you to come up with an excuse."

"*Bandstand*," Roxanne explained, "gives a young girl like yourself a productive, creative outlet where you can develop leadership skills, grow as an individual, and be a role model for all of America. What kind of role model would you be if you didn't honor your commitments and obligations?" Meg took in Roxanne's explanation, somewhat impressed, knowing that soon she'd be repeating that line verbatim to her dad. "Am I right or am I right? That was good, huh?" Roxanne asked, proud of her compelling argument. Meg couldn't really argue; Roxanne had a point, even if it was to facilitate a devious plan.

"I hate lying," Meg said, collapsing onto her bed. She knew the outcome was inevitable. Either way her parents weren't going to hear the truth.

"You'll hate missing the Beatles concert more,"

Roxanne reminded her. Meg pulled the covers over her head. She didn't want to admit it, but she knew full well that Roxanne was right.

"It's a place for me to develop leadership skills," Meg said, pleading her case to her mother, who was transferring laundry from the washing machine to the dryer. "Where I can grow and be a role model . . ." Meg struggled to remember Roxanne's quote and wished she'd had the good sense to write it down.

"And it's her responsibility," Roxanne chimed in, standing next to Meg for moral support.

"To whom?" Helen asked.

"Her fans," replied Roxanne simply. Meg looked at Roxanne, marveling at how good she was at coming up with these things. "All the regulars are required to attend," Roxanne continued, lying on Meg's behalf. "Right, Meg?" she asked encouragingly.

Meg hesitated for a moment but realized it was now or never. And besides, there were sins worse than lying—like adultery or murdering someone. All Meg wanted to do was see the Beatles. *Really,* she convinced herself, *what's the sin in that?*

"If we don't go, we get kicked off the show," Meg added convincingly. "It's really important. For the future of *Bandstand.*"

"And America!" Roxanne chimed in, going slightly overboard, as usual.

"And it's tomorrow?" Helen confirmed, wary about the details. She turned on the dryer.

"We'd meet Michael Brooks at WFIL in the morning and all caravan to the shore. And we'd be back tomorrow night," Roxanne explained.

"And Michael Brooks?" Helen asked. "You'd be with him the whole time?"

Meg nodded, adding, "He's in charge of the whole thing."

"Because you can't go without adult supervision," Helen said. Meg suddenly felt ten years old again.

"We'd be with him the whole time," Roxanne assured Helen. "There's absolutely nothing to worry about."

Helen asked pointedly, "Who exactly would be doing the driving?"

"I would," Meg piped up. Helen did a double take, trying unsuccessfully to cover her horror. The bashed-in mailbox had just been replaced that morning.

"Hon, you just got your license," Helen responded in disbelief, wondering how Meg would be so bold as to ask for something of this magnitude. "You're still getting comfortable driving around Philly."

"That's not fair!" Meg protested. "My license is to drive. Not just drive in Philly."

"Hon—," Helen began.

Meg quickly interrupted. "What good was getting my license if I can't go anywhere?" she pointed out, exasperated.

"But it's so far . . . ," Helen said. "Too far."

"You let JJ drive there yesterday!" Meg countered, her voice rising to a pitch that only Mrs. Kirby's dog next door could hear. JJ and Beth had left yesterday for Beth's parents' beach house just north of Wildwood. Beth had been as angry at JJ as Helen was for joining the marines without consulting anyone. And although JJ couldn't seem to do anything to appease his mother's anger, he hoped that spending some quality time alone with Beth would at least mend things between them.

Roxanne grabbed Meg's arm, reminding her to keep calm. Meg lowered her voice, trying to maintain her cool.

"JJ is different," explained Helen. "He's been driving a lot longer than you have."

"It's always different with JJ," complained Meg. "He gets to do whatever he wants. Spend the night at Beth's, go to the shore anytime he wants, borrow

Dad's car . . . I can't even spend the day at the beach for *Bandstand*."

"That's not true," Helen said, more because she felt she had to say it than because she believed it. There was a double standard for JJ in the Pryor household, a standard Helen wasn't entirely comfortable with. It seemed that Jack let JJ get away with the same things for which he would typically ground Meg. Although Helen could never admit it, Meg was right. It wasn't fair.

"I'll talk to your father," Helen relented. "But I can't promise anything." Meg smiled and wrapped her arms around her mother, thrilled that she was inching her way closer to seeing John, Paul, George, and Ringo. Roxanne looked at her and winked.

That night Meg sat at the bottom of the attic stairs and listened as her parents argued in their bedroom. It had been going on for well over an hour, and Meg couldn't tell if any progress was being made at all.

"Jack," Helen argued, "at some point we have to trust her."

"The way you get trust, Helen," Jack countered, "is you earn it."

Helen was growing exasperated and raising her

voice. "We can't keep her locked in this house forever."

"The riot is just winding down. Who's to say it couldn't start back up?" Jack argued. "It's not safe out there."

Helen agreed, saying, "It would probably be safer for her there than here." Jack didn't say anything. "She's been locked in this house—"

Jack interrupted. "Locked in this house?" he yelled. "C'mon, Helen. I let her take that driver's test, I know she went to *Bandstand* the past two days, you told me Roxanne was up in that attic all afternoon. . . . After her getting stuck in that riot, I think I'm being pretty easy on her."

"You know how much this means to her," Helen pleaded. "If she doesn't go, she doesn't get to dance on the show." Meg cringed, knowing that part was a lie. She felt awful letting her mother defend something that wasn't true—but what was the alternative? Sometimes she felt that because her dad was so strict, it forced her to go to desperate measures. Why couldn't he just trust her judgment and let her make her own decisions?

"Would that be such a bad thing?" Jack asked.

Helen softened. "Jack, she saw someone shot. Maybe killed. She's been through a terrible ordeal. If dancing on that show makes her feel better . . . why not?" Meg strained to hear her dad's response, but Patty appeared on the stairs.

"This seems awfully convenient," Patty pointed out.

"Shut up, Patty," Meg said out of habit.

"It's pretty coincidental that this *Bandstand* thing just happens to be on the same day as the Beatles concert."

"So what?" Meg asked, not giving anything away but fearing Patty would figure out the truth. Luckily her parents hadn't. The Beatles' summer tour wasn't exactly on their pop culture radar. However, Patty was a whole different story. Meg darted her eyes around nervously as her sister continued. Patty was a lot like the sun—you didn't want to look at her directly.

"I can't help but notice that Wildwood is only an hour from Atlantic City," Patty added pointedly. "And that the Beatles are playing there tomorrow night."

"So what?" Meg said defensively. "Dad already said no to the concert."

"But I'm sure he'd be interested to know that it's tomorrow—the same day as the hop. Coincidence?" Patty was on to her. Meg knew there was no looking back.

"What do you want, Patty?" Meg asked. "Money?"

Patty considered for a moment. "Your blue cashmere sweater," she said. "The one Beth gave you."

"I love that sweater!" Meg cried.

Patty considered her options. "And . . ."

"And?" Meg said, incredulous. Her little sister was unbelievable.

"John Lennon's autograph," she answered matter-of-factly.

Meg scoffed at the absurdity of the request. "Patty, how am I supposed to get John Lennon's autograph?"

"You get that, I won't tell."

"That's impossible!" Meg complained.

"You've figured everything else out." Patty shrugged. "I'm sure you'll find a way to pull it off." She walked away, satisfied with herself, leaving Meg to wonder what her parents would decide—and how exactly she would get John Lennon's autograph if they agreed to let her go.

Twelve hours later Jack was nervously handing his guilt-ridden sixteen-year-old daughter the car keys. Why couldn't she be one of those girls who didn't have a conscience, like Roxanne?

"Meg," he said. "You—"

"Drive carefully," she finished. "I know."

Jack poured the pressure on. "I'm trusting you, Meg. Don't mess this up for yourself." Meg gulped, trying to cover up the fact that in the excitement of getting permission to drive the car to Wildwood, she'd overlooked one key component of this road trip: She was actually going to have to drive to Wildwood. Just then a knock at the door interrupted her mounting panic.

"Roxanne's here!" Meg said, pushing any trepidation about the impending road trip out of her thoughts. She ran for the door and threw it open, revealing Luke.

Quickly Meg stepped out onto the porch, shutting the door behind her. "You can't be here," she whispered.

"What're you talking about?" Luke asked, not realizing that when Meg had called him late last night saying she could go, she'd left out a big part of the story. Like the part about not telling her dad about the Beatles concert. And the part about not telling her dad that Luke was coming. "He doesn't know I'm going?"

"Well, you're so . . . vocal . . . about how much you hate *Bandstand*," Meg explained. "My dad would never have believed you were spending all that time in the car just to watch *Bandstand* live."

"But what about the concert?" Luke asked, not sure he wanted to be a part of a scheme concocted by Meg and Roxanne.

"I'll explain later," Meg said nervously. "You have to hide." She was sure she was on the brink of getting caught.

Jack yelled from inside. "Meg?"

Panicked, Meg ushered Luke down the stairs. "Go wait on the corner," she said, leading him to the front walk. "Go!" she whispered urgently as Luke took off running.

"Meg . . ." Jack opened the door and looked around suspiciously. "What's going on out here?"

Meg struggled to think of an excuse, wondering what the equivalent was for wrong number. "Wrong house?" she said, knowing it was yet another pathetic lie.

While Jack busied himself inspecting the car, Helen handed Meg bag lunches she'd made for her and Roxanne.

"I hope Roxanne likes bologna," Helen said.

"I do!" Roxanne piped in as she entered through the mudroom door. She looked at her watch. "We'd better get going. In case there's traffic on the interstate," she said knowingly, repeating the line

Meg's father said every summer when they packed to go down to the shore. Meg laughed to herself. Roxanne, the queen of public transportation, had never driven a day in her life and didn't know the first thing about interstates and traffic.

"Meg, do you have a map?" Helen asked.

"In the glove compartment," Meg said by rote. She and Jack had gone over this earlier.

"Car looks good," he said, entering from outside.

"Good morning, Mr. Pryor," Roxanne said sweetly. Jack mumbled a hello, not in the mood to deal with Roxanne. He knew it was Roxanne who had probably given Meg the idea to borrow his car.

"And you have the number at Beth's parents' house?" Helen questioned.

"Memorized," Meg replied.

"You call here every three hours," Jack demanded. "And as soon as the *Bandstand* thing is over, you come home. No discussion." Meg looked at Roxanne out of the corner of her eye, knowing that was hardly what they had planned. Roxanne jumped in before Meg's guilty expression gave anything away.

"You got it, Mr. Pryor." Roxanne nodded. "Every three hours."

"On the dot," Jack reiterated. "And Meg?"

"Yes?" she said.

"If you're late, if anything happens," he said slowly, hitting each word with precision, "that's it." Meg didn't even ask what "that's it" meant—she knew it wasn't good.

"Don't worry," she said, smiling through gritted teeth to cover a severe sense of dread. "Nothing will happen." Subtly, so that no one would notice, Meg balled up one fist and knocked on the wooden kitchen table. She wasn't normally superstitious, but when it came to her dad's car and Roxanne's crazy plan, she needed all the help she could get.

Eight

Aside from a little confusion over fifth gear and reverse in the Pryor garage (Jack couldn't even watch her back out), a heated argument between Luke and Roxanne about which radio station to listen to (Meg, who sided with Roxanne, had the deciding vote), and a little confusion with the map (it flew out the window while Roxanne was trying to read it), their trip was relatively uneventful.

They made it to Wildwood Pier with about twenty minutes to spare, which gave a group of screaming teenage fans enough time to encircle their car. "Oh my gosh!" a teenage girl screamed. "It's Meg. From Meg and Jimmy."

Even though Jimmy Riley had been off *Bandstand* for months, fans still thought of them as a couple. "Should I tell them it's actually Meg and *Luke* now?" Luke asked a little sullenly.

"There's Roxanne," another girl pointed out. "Roxanne!" she called. "Over here!" As Roxanne waved to her fans, Meg turned to Luke.

"You can't say anything, Luke," Meg said. "They'd hate me for dating someone so soon after Jimmy. It'd be practically like cheating," she explained.

"You really can't cheat on a fictional boyfriend," Luke pointed out.

"For the next few hours," Meg explained, "consider me single." Luke cringed. He didn't like the sound of that. "But after *Bandstand,*" Meg added sweetly, "I'm all yours." It didn't quite make sense to Luke, but for once he decided not to argue. This was Meg's birthday celebration, after all, and he wanted her to have a good time.

"Ready?" Roxanne asked as Meg took the keys out of the ignition.

Meg looked at Roxanne happily. "Look at all these people!" she said in disbelief.

"You'd think we were the Beatles or something," Roxanne commented.

Luke rolled his eyes. Meg and Roxanne may have been semifamous local television personalities, but they were definitely *not* the Beatles. "Keep dreaming, Roxanne," Luke muttered under his breath, but loud enough for Roxanne to get riled up.

"Don't be jealous, Luke," Roxanne shot back, "just because no one's asking for your autograph."

Meg pleaded with both of them. "You guys. Not another fight."

Aside from their half-hour argument about which station to listen to on the drive down, Luke and Roxanne had also bickered about who got to ride shotgun and where to stop for food. Meg reminded her friends, "We're here to have fun, remember?" She made Luke and Roxanne agree to a temporary truce for the remainder of the day.

With that, the Three Musketeers, as Roxanne had dubbed them upon declaring the truce, got out of the car. Two of the three were swarmed by overly enthusiastic fans, who followed them all the way from the parking lot to the pier, asking for photos and autographs. And the other Musketeer, the one with wide-rimmed glasses and a distinctly unteenage taste in music, lingered in the background, realizing, perhaps for the very first time, that although his girlfriend was no Beatle, she was definitely, undeniably famous.

The hop turned out to be a huge success. Performers that were wary of coming to Philly were more than willing to drive to the nearby Jersey Shore instead. Hundreds of people, including Luke, surrounded the makeshift *Bandstand* set on the pier near the boardwalk, trying to get a look at Dick Clark and the various musical guests. The crowd went wild when he introduced the Kinks as the opening act. After more performances by Dave Clark Five, Martha and the Vandellas, and the Gentrys, Dick Clark played "Can't Buy Me Love," by the Beatles, and the dance floor erupted. Roxanne reminded Meg that in a few short hours they wouldn't just be hearing their song, they'd be seeing them live.

When they found Luke after the show, he was sitting on a wooden bench on the pier, drinking a strawberry Slushee and talking to a pretty girl with long blond hair. To make things even worse, this girl, who had the longest legs Meg had ever seen, was wearing nothing but a wide-rimmed straw hat and a bikini.

"What does he think he's doing?" Meg asked, horrified. She watched as Luke said something and the girl laughed. Judging by her reaction, whatever he said must have been hilarious.

"I'm sure whatever he said," Roxanne noted, "wasn't *that* funny."

"Is he . . . ," Meg said, squinting at the girl, convinced it was a mistake, "actually flirting?" From Meg's experience Luke's version of flirting was based upon completely annoying the object of his affection, and definitely not making her laugh.

Roxanne put her hand on Meg's shoulder. "Easy, killer." Undeterred, Meg marched over to Luke. Roxanne reluctantly followed.

"Hi, Luke," Meg said accusingly. Luke looked up.

"Oh, Meg," he responded, sounding somewhat surprised. "I didn't think you'd be finished so soon."

Roxanne chimed in. "Clearly." The girl shifted uncomfortably, looking at Luke.

"This is Carrie," he said, introducing his new friend. "Carrie, this is Meg and Roxanne." Meg raised her eyebrows. Surely Luke was going to give more of an introduction than that.

"*And?*" Roxanne asked, giving Luke a not-so-subtle hint.

"And," Luke added, "Meg is my girlfriend, and Roxanne's her best friend, who seems to be permanently attached to her side." Luke smiled smugly at Roxanne, satisfied with his answer and his not-so-subtle insult.

"Huh," Carrie replied, seemingly disappointed to discover that Luke wasn't single. "You didn't mention you had a girlfriend." Meg looked at Luke, but before she could muster up a witty response, she and Roxanne were swarmed by a group of teenage girls begging for autographs.

Meg and Roxanne obliged as Luke explained to

Carrie, "They dance on *American Bandstand.*" Carrie wasn't very impressed.

"I'm not really a big fan," she admitted. Luke smiled. A kindred spirit. Meg looked up from signing a T-shirt, horrified. This girl was pretty, blond, *and* a *Bandstand* hater. She met all of Luke's qualifications for a perfect girlfriend. All she had to do now was express an inexplicable love for Bob Dylan, and Meg would have to toss her over the pier. Or get Roxanne to push her off. Luckily, by the time Meg finished signing autographs—she'd even signed one boy's arm—Carrie and her long legs were nowhere to be found.

"What?" As if nothing unusual had just happened, Luke shrugged innocently, acting as if sharing a strawberry Slushee with a pretty girl wearing nothing but a hat and a bikini were a daily occurrence, as common as brushing his teeth or tying his shoes. "What about all those guys surrounding you?" Luke pointed out. "You don't see me getting mad."

"Those are my fans!" Meg said, defending herself.

Luke gestured to the spot on the park bench where Carrie had been sitting. "Well, I have a fan too," he said with a laugh. "Carrie." Meg didn't crack a smile. "C'mon, Meg," Luke ribbed her. "You wouldn't want me to disappoint her, would you? My one and only fan?"

As Meg contemplated her response Roxanne turned to the few lingering *Bandstand* fans. "So sorry, but we have to go now," she said, grabbing Meg's hand. She waved her concert ticket at the fans. "You see, we have a very important date with four guys from Liverpool in Atlantic City," she explained, "and we can't be—"

"Be what?" a familiar male voice asked. Meg and Roxanne spun around and found themselves face-to-face with JJ and his girlfriend, Beth.

"JJ!" Meg exclaimed, surprised, a familiar feeling forming in the pit of her stomach. How much had he heard? And had he already seen that she was here with—

"Luke," JJ said, extending his hand. Luke stepped forward and shook it. Meg gulped. Too late.

"It's funny," JJ said, feigning confusion. "I thought just you and Roxanne were coming down. For the hop."

Roxanne thought quickly. "Luke drove down here on his own," she said. "You know, to surprise her."

Meg went along with it. "Yeah," she said, nodding.

She didn't want to lie to JJ, but she felt like she'd dug herself in so deep she had no choice.

Roxanne added, "Luke's always doing sweet things like that, aren't you, Luke?"

Luke nodded in agreement. "All the time," he answered, trying to sound as convincing as possible.

"Luke's amazing that way," Roxanne reiterated. "He's the best boyfriend. In fact, I don't know why I'm not dating him." Roxanne smiled, twirling her hair with her finger. "Maybe because I've always had a crush on you, JJ." Roxanne shrugged. "You're so compassionate and understanding." Meg shot Roxanne a look, and Roxanne remembered that Beth was standing right there. "No offense, Beth."

Beth smiled, amused. "None taken, Roxanne."

"Save it, Roxanne," JJ warned, not buying any of it. "And what's this?" he asked, casually grabbing the Beatles ticket out of Roxanne's hand.

"I have no idea," she claimed, feigning innocence. "A fan just gave it to me to sign." Roxanne looked over JJ's shoulder as if she was just as curious about what it said. "Huh," she said, reading. "How odd."

JJ had had enough. "Okay, you guys, let's stop pretending," he said. "You're going to the concert.

And Dad has no idea." Meg felt herself cracking under her brother's accusations. She couldn't take lying to JJ, of all people.

"JJ," Meg begged. "Please don't say anything. He'll kill me. Well, he'll ground me again . . . and then he'll kill me."

"Meg—," JJ began.

"Luke and Roxanne got the tickets for my birthday, and Dad wouldn't let me go because he's being such a jerk," Meg complained.

"He wouldn't let you go because it's Atlantic City," JJ explained. "Meg, you're only sixteen."

"You and Beth went on a road trip when you were sixteen," Meg shot back, reminding him of the time he and Beth drove to Delaware when they were in high school.

"Look," JJ said, suddenly pitying her. He knew how hard it was to have to answer to their dad all the time. "I won't say anything unless they ask. But you be careful. And if you're not home by midnight, I'm telling them." Roxanne and Meg happily hugged him and quickly took off for the car. Luke looked at JJ as if to say, *Women!* and hurriedly followed after them. It looked like nothing could stop them.

"Meg," JJ called after her, "don't forget to call Dad." But by that time they were long gone. He shook his head at Beth, resigned to the fact that Meg hadn't heard a word he'd said.

"Dad?" Meg said into a pay phone. She had called him once quickly before *Bandstand* started. He'd been relieved to know she'd made it to Wildwood safely. This was call number two. On the other end of the phone Jack asked if it was a bad connection.

"No, it's not that," she yelled. "I can barely hear you." Despite the large knot that was growing in her stomach, she motioned for Roxanne to turn the radio up. "Dave Clark Five is playing." That wasn't really a lie—Dave Clark Five *was* playing . . . on the radio, at least. Roxanne cranked up the volume on the radio, and she and Luke screamed overlapping screams of "I love you" and "We love Dave Clark Five," trying to sound like a crowd of overzealous fans. It sounded terrible. Meg gestured, silently silencing them. They stopped yelling but kept the car radio blaring.

"Everything's good," she said, "but Michael Brooks . . . he asked us to stay for a little while longer."

"Night show," Roxanne whispered, coaxing her.

"They're gonna do a night show under the

lights," Meg lied quickly, to make it less painful.

"For needy children," Roxanne added, trying to make the lie sound good.

Meg gave her a horrified look, then reluctantly said, "For needy children." Meg had an awful feeling they both were going straight to hell for that lie. She covered the receiver with her hand.

"The second we get back, I'm driving us both to confession," Meg whispered adamantly. She put her ear back up to the phone, listening to her father, and then went sheet white. "You want to talk to who?" she asked, her voice shaking slightly. She hoped she had misheard her father's request. "No, no," she covered. "Hold on . . . let me get him." Meg covered the receiver with her hand.

"He wants to talk to Michael," she whispered, panicked, then bit her bottom lip. Both girls looked immediately at Luke. He backed up, throwing his hands into the air.

"No way," Luke said. "*No way.*"

Roxanne pleaded. "Luke," she said, "you're the only one here with a semimasculine voice." Luke looked at her, incredulous.

"What exactly are you implying about the other half of my voice?" Luke asked defensively.

"This isn't all about you!" Roxanne exclaimed.

"Do it for Paul. Do it for Ringo." Roxanne leaned in dramatically. "Do it for Meg."

"No . . . no . . . no," Luke protested, until Roxanne grabbed the receiver and shoved it up to Luke's ear.

"Hello?" Luke said, clearing his voice and lowering it. "Mr. Pryor? Um . . . Michael . . ." He looked hopelessly at Meg for Michael's last name.

"Brooks!" Meg and Roxanne whispered simultaneously.

"Brooks here," Luke continued. "You wanted to speak with me?" He waited a moment, listening to Jack. His heart was pounding out of his chest. He didn't even like the Beatles that much. If this wasn't love—driving in a car with Meg at the wheel, attending a *Bandstand* hop, and lying to Meg's father—he didn't know what was.

"No, sir," Luke said, clearing his throat again. "I'm older than I sound. Um . . ." He looked at Meg and Roxanne for help.

"Twenty-six!" they both said, jumping up and down with nervousness.

"Twenty-six," Luke answered, dodging another bullet, although he wondered if Jack would really know the difference. "We're asking our regular dancers to stay for a special *Bandstand* event under the lights," he continued. "A couple of performers came down to sing for the . . ."

"Needy children!" Meg and Roxanne whispered. Meg was certain. They were going to hell.

"Who's singing?" Luke asked, looking to the girls.

"Brenda Lee," Meg fired back.

"Peggy Lee," Roxanne suggested.

"It's kind of a Lee theme," Luke improvised. "Brenda Lee, Peggy Lee . . ." And then, getting into the lie, he added with a flourish, "Sara Lee . . ." Meg and Roxanne looked at each other, eyes wide with horror. Did Luke really just say "Sara Lee"?

"Sara Lee's a snack cake," Roxanne spit. "Not a singer!" She punched Luke in the arm.

"Ow!" Luke yelled. He quickly recovered and responded to Jack, "No, no sir. I'm fine. One of the dancers just . . . fell off the stage . . . and slammed into the phone booth." Looking to the girls for help, Luke realized he was going down fast. "I'll have Meg home as soon as we're done." He listened for a second. "Yes," he agreed. "By ten. You have a good day, Mr. Pryor." Luke hung up, breathing a huge sigh of relief. Lying had been so strenuous that he'd begun to sweat. Or, he realized, maybe it wasn't the pressure of lying that made him sweat. It was being under the burning gazes of Meg and Roxanne for saying "Sara Lee."

Nine

It took a minute for it to register that Meg was in serious trouble. If the loud crash weren't indication enough, the driver yelling in front of her let her know without a shadow of a doubt that she'd rear-ended his car.

"What the hell?" the driver screamed, getting out and slamming his car door hard. He didn't seem much older than they were; he looked about nineteen or twenty, tops. He inspected his back bumper.

Only five minutes away from the concert venue, they were so close that a moment ago Meg swore she could almost hear the Beatles singing. Or maybe that was Roxanne in the backseat. Either way, now all Meg could hear was the sound of her heart pounding as she sat absolutely frozen in the driver's seat, a look of terror etched on her face.

"Oh my gosh," she cried. "Did I really just . . ." She knew the answer was yes. "Oh my gosh. My dad is going to kill me."

"Meg," Roxanne assured her. "It wasn't your

fault. Did you see how suddenly he stopped?"
Roxanne was right—the driver *had* stopped suddenly. Admittedly, Meg was driving a little faster
than normal to get there. When the car ahead of her
made the quick decision to fly through the yellow
light at an intersection, Meg followed. And when he
made an even more last-minute decision to stop,
Luke's yelling gave her time to slam on her brakes
and slow down significantly before she hit the car
ahead. Clearly the man had been driving erratically,
confusing the people around him. Surely that could
not have been her fault.

Luke gave Roxanne, who had never driven a car
in her life—at least not legally—the bad news. "She
hit him from behind," he stated. "If you rear-end
someone, it's always your fault." With all hope gone
of laying the blame elsewhere, Meg's eyes filled
with tears.

"Luke!" Roxanne said, agitated. "You're not
helping!"

Bam, bam, bam! The other driver pounded on
Meg's window, startling her. Fumbling for the door
handle, Meg nervously got out of the car. Luke and
Roxanne joined her for moral support.

"I am so sorry," Meg apologized to the other
driver. "It's all completely my fault."

"You need to look where you're going," he shot back rudely, beginning a screaming rant about what a bad driver she was, how she should look where she's going, how they were letting anybody on the road these days. . . .

As Meg politely listened she dug her fingernails into the palm of her hand to keep from crying. Nearby, Luke inspected their car for possible damage and found that one side of the bumper had crashed to the ground.

"This can't be good," Luke mumbled under his breath.

"I've never been in an accident before," Meg told the driver. "In fact, I just got my license a few days ago."

"Figures," the driver muttered under his breath. Then he said, "I'll need your license and registration."

Meg had no idea where the registration even was. "Um . . . ," she stammered. "I'm not . . . sure . . . um . . ."

"And I'll need your home phone number," he added. Meg's eyes widened. There was no way she was letting this guy call her house. If he did, she could kiss her license good-bye . . . and probably *Bandstand* . . . and probably Luke . . . and probably anything else she loved that her dad could threaten to take away. She threw a desperate glance at Roxanne.

Roxanne stepped forward. "I'm sorry," she said to the driver. "I didn't catch your name."

"Ryan," he said drily, uninterested in making small talk.

"Hi, Ryan," Roxanne said, then gave introductions all around. "I'm Roxanne. This is Meg. And over there is our friend Luke." Luke waved, then turned his attention back to Meg's bumper, hoisting it off the ground.

"By any chance," Roxanne continued, "do you watch *American Bandstand*?"

Ryan looked at her like she was crazy. "What?" he asked, caught off guard, unsure how the TV show related to the car accident.

"You know, *American Bandstand*," Roxanne tried again. "Popular show, Dick Clark, musical guests, talented not to mention good-looking dancers . . ."

Ryan shrugged. "I think my girlfriend and all her friends watch it. Why?"

Roxanne's eyes lit up. "Because Meg, here, and I," she explained, "we're dancers on the show. Regulars." She continued to work her magic. "Maybe your girlfriend would like an autograph . . . ," she hinted.

"From you two?" Ryan scoffed. "No."

"From whomever," she said casually. "You name it. Brenda Lee, Shirley Ellis, Jay and the Americans, Martha and . . . all those Vandellas."

Ryan shook his head. "The only autograph my girlfriend wants is Paul McCartney's." He corrected himself. "Well, ex-girlfriend."

Roxanne took this information in. "Ex-girlfriend," she said, suddenly interested. "So you're saying you're available?" She took one step closer. Maybe this would be easier than she thought.

"I like blondes," Ryan said, stopping her.

Roxanne raised her eyebrows. "Your loss," she said, quickly deciding to change her tack. "So why ex-girlfriend? What'd you do?" she asked bluntly.

"None of your business," he said defensively.

"She dumped you?" Roxanne guessed.

Ryan's ego couldn't take that accusation. "She caught me kissing her best friend."

"What?" Roxanne and Meg exclaimed in unison.

Ryan threw up his hands defensively. "I already got an earful from her . . . I don't need it from the two of you." He looked at Meg again. "Are you getting your registration, or what?"

Roxanne quickly jumped in, distracting him. "You know what would be better than an autograph from Paul McCartney?" Roxanne asked.

"Never having kissed her best friend," Ryan said thoughtfully.

"Seeing Paul McCartney *live*," Roxanne suggested, turning to Meg. "Where's your Beatles ticket?"

Meg hesitated, afraid of where this was going. "In my purse," she answered slowly. Roxanne opened the car door and grabbed Meg's purse. She fished out the concert ticket and waved the ticket in front of Ryan.

"Take this," she said. "As payment for any damage to your car."

"Roxanne—wait!" Meg gasped, her eyes widening.

"Meg, it's only fair," Roxanne said. She turned toward Ryan. "You give this ticket to your girlfriend, and I guarantee . . . she won't care if you make out with her sister," Roxanne said convincingly. "And as far as this little car thing, we call it even."

"Are you serious?" Ryan asked, pleased.

Roxanne nodded. "Dead serious."

Ryan considered for a moment. He walked over and inspected his own car. Aside from the bumper being a little marked up and the license plate dented, there was no other damage.

Ryan shrugged and walked back to Roxanne. "You've got a deal." Roxanne smiled broadly and handed him the ticket. Ryan looked at it in disbelief.

"She's gonna love me for this," he said happily. "Meg and Roxanne, was it?" The girls nodded. "Thanks."

Ryan laughed ruefully as he walked toward his car. "It's my dad's car anyway," he said to himself with a shrug, happy with the outcome. The car didn't mean that much to him in the first place.

Luke looked up from trying to repair Meg's bumper, surprised that Ryan was leaving so easily and quickly. "Take care, man," Luke said with a wave. He was curious about what exactly had transpired between all parties involved.

After Ryan drove away, Meg turned around, upset with Roxanne. "How could you give away my ticket?" she cried.

"I didn't give away your ticket!" Roxanne argued.

Meg held up her purse and shoved the contents in Roxanne's face. "No ticket!"

Roxanne relented. "Okay, fine. If you want to be technical, I gave away your ticket," she admitted. "But don't worry. You're still going to the concert."

"How?" Meg asked, exasperated.

Roxanne smiled. She was, as usual, a girl with a plan. "You'll use Luke's," she said, shrugging.

As if on cue, Luke gave one more forceful shove

to the bumper and lodged it back in place. Proudly he stood up and looked at Roxanne and Meg, who were both staring at him, dreading telling him the bad news.

"What?" Luke asked, looking around nervously.

Roxanne looked at Meg, who took a deep breath.

"Do you want the good news or the bad news first?" Meg asked, knowing Luke was about to be very upset.

"I'm *not* upset," Luke insisted for the twentieth time as they parked the car at the Atlantic City Convention Hall. Meg wished they had arrived earlier so they could have enjoyed the boardwalk, full of stands serving everything from hot dogs and pizza to saltwater taffy and cotton candy. To three hungry teenagers it sounded like the perfect well-balanced meal. Meg turned off the ignition but didn't get out of the car. She turned to Luke.

"Are you sure?" Meg asked, feeling like the biggest jerk in the world. "You're not upset?"

"Chop-chop, people," Roxanne reminded them as she climbed out of the car and slammed the door. "The concert's starting."

Meg felt the guilt eating away at her. "I feel terrible," she said.

Luke shrugged. "Don't feel bad now. Feel bad when I'm washing Mr. Greenwood's car for the twenty-second Saturday in a row for the Beatles concert I didn't get to see."

Meg thrust a ticket back to Luke. "Here, take this," she said, surrendering the ticket. "You go and have fun." Luke appreciated the gesture, but he closed her outstretched fingers back into a fist around the ticket.

"Meg," he said sincerely, "this is for you. For your birthday. You love the Beatles. Now, go. Enjoy. I'm sure I can find a way to occupy my time for the next few hours."

Meg's heart swelled with emotion. This was her chance. Her chance to tell him everything—how much he meant to her, how much she loved him. Those three little words were hovering on the tip of her tongue, just waiting to be spoken.

"Luke," she began, excited at the prospect of telling him how she felt. "I . . . I—"

"Am about to make us late for the concert," Roxanne interrupted as she threw open the driver's side door and yanked Meg out of the car. Luke hopped out as well.

"All right, all right," Meg said. "I'm coming!" Roxanne took off running for the main entrance while Meg lingered a moment longer.

"What were you going to say?" Luke asked. Meg thought for a second, regretting that the moment had passed.

"Just . . . thanks," she said, and gave him a big hug.

The lobby of the convention hall was a frenzied mob scene, the air thick with excitement. The crowd was electric with the anticipation of seeing their favorite band. Thousands of people were packed in, pushing their way to their seats. Meg and Roxanne held hands to prevent getting separated from each other, but even so, they lost each other twice. It took more than half an hour just to get to their row, not only because of the thousands of people ahead of them, but also because their seats could not have been any farther from the stage. As bad luck would have it, they were in the very last row.

"This can't be right," Roxanne complained, checking the ticket to see if somehow she'd misread it. "Who was Mr. Greenwood's big connection? The janitor?"

Meg checked hers as well, comparing it with the seat numbers. They were definitely in the right place. The lights started to fade as the girls slipped into their subpar seats. Even in the last row, however, Meg's enthusiasm could not be dimmed. She was at the Beatles concert. In minutes she would be in the same time and space as her idols, listening to them play. She felt like the luckiest girl in the world.

Next to them, in what was supposed to be Luke's seat, a girl was screaming her guts out, chanting, "I love you, John! I love you, Paul! I love you, George!"

"What about Ringo?" Roxanne mumbled defensively to Meg. She loved Ringo.

The screaming girl next to them had to be Ryan's girlfriend, but with the concert starting and the screaming all around them reaching a fever pitch, they escaped awkward small talk.

"Ladies and gentlemen," a voice boomed through the arena. "John Lennon, Paul McCartney, George Harrison, and Ringo Starr—the Beatles!"

From the moment the Beatles appeared onstage, from the first strum of their guitars playing the introduction to "I Want to Hold Your Hand," the crowd exploded. The Beatles began singing, and the crowd erupted into shrieks and cheers. However, much to Roxanne's Ringo-obsessed dismay, a large column was blocking her view of the stage.

"Oh yeah, I'll tell you something," the Beatles sang. "I think you'll understand."

As Roxanne shuffled to find a new spot Meg bounced up and down, singing along, screaming the lyrics at the top of her lungs with the rest of the audience. "When l say that something . . . I wanna hold your hand!"

Meg turned to Roxanne. "This is incredible!" she yelled. "Rox, thank you so much." Sadly, Roxanne's enthusiasm was greatly diminished by her inability to see the stage.

"What's wrong?" Meg screamed in Roxanne's ear. When Roxanne explained that her view of the stage was blocked, Meg suggested she switch with Ryan's girlfriend.

"*Ex*-girlfriend," Roxanne corrected her.

"I mean," reasoned Meg, "it *was* our seat."

"Excuse me," yelled Roxanne, reaching across Meg to tug on the sleeve of Ryan's ex-girlfriend. She didn't get much further than that. The girl not only refused Roxanne's request, she threatened to have Ryan call Meg's dad about the accident if Roxanne refused to leave her alone.

Desperate, Roxanne made a rash decision. She turned to Meg, who was busy singing her heart out, jumping up and down like a crazed fan. "And when

I touch you, I feel happy inside. It's such a feeling that my love I can't hide . . . I can't hide . . . ," Meg screamed, throwing her arms above her head in pure Beatles bliss, "I CAN'T HIDE!"

Roxanne grabbed her arm. "Grab your stuff, Meg."

"What?" Meg asked, astonished, suddenly shaken from her reverie. *Roxanne surely doesn't think we're leaving!* she thought. "Where are we going?"

"To get better seats," Roxanne responded. She pulled Meg out into the aisle as they made their way toward the door.

"Roxanne, wait," Meg pleaded. "It's sold out. There aren't any better seats. We're going to miss the concert." Roxanne tightened her grip on Meg's hand. Either the concert was so loud that she couldn't hear a thing, or Roxanne was just ignoring Meg. Either way Meg's protests fell on deaf ears.

By the time they got to the lobby, Meg could hear the final lines of "I Want to Hold Your Hand." She heard John's voice thanking the crowd for coming out.

A few feet from them a medic was trying to revive a girl who had fainted with excitement. Meg wished one of the medics would examine Roxanne's head. Surely she'd lost her mind.

"Wait right here," Roxanne instructed, taking Meg's ticket. "I'll be right back."

Meg tried to reason with her. "Roxanne," she said, trying not to freak out completely. "How on earth are we going to get better seats?"

Roxanne held Meg's face in her hands. "Meg, we're celebrities," Roxanne reminded her. "They have special seats for people like us. People on TV." Meg wasn't so sure. Roxanne could see the look of doubt creeping onto her friend's face. "Trust me," she said.

And before Meg could get another word out, Roxanne was gone.

An hour later Roxanne still hadn't returned. Meg had started to feel angry within twenty minutes of Roxanne's hasty departure. Now she was so furious she couldn't even see straight. From the lobby she'd already missed four of her favorite songs—"Can't Buy Me Love," "All My Loving," "I Saw Her Standing There," and "Twist and Shout." As the Beatles launched into "Please Please Me," Meg's heart was pounding and beating so fast she felt as if she might explode at any moment.

It wouldn't have been so bad if Roxanne hadn't taken her ticket. Then she could have just gone back to her supposedly crappy seat, which had a distant but perfectly good view of the stage, and enjoyed the rest of the show. Instead she was stuck in the lobby, counting the number of people receiving medical attention. So far eleven girls had fainted, seven girls had received treatment for trample-related injuries, and if Meg got her hands on her, she knew of at least one dark-haired ticket-snatching Beatles fan who was going to be in critical condition once she finally returned from attempting to upgrade their seats.

Meg had already tried to convince the guy at the door to let her back in.

"I don't know if you recognize me," she'd said, dying of embarrassment that she was actually trying something so ridiculous. "I'm Meg. From *American Bandstand*?"

But the guy had just looked at her blankly and said, "Sorry, kid. I don't care if you're Elvis Presley. You need a ticket, just like everyone else."

A half hour later Roxanne returned. Her hair was messy and her lipstick was smudged, but all Meg noticed was that ninety minutes of the concert had passed—without her!

"Where have you been?" Meg screamed,

controlling every natural impulse she had to jump on Roxanne and tackle her to the ground. "We missed the whole concert. They're on the second encore."

"No, no," Roxanne corrected. "I saw it. Backstage."

"You WHAT?" Meg shouted, enraged.

Roxanne grabbed her shoulders and looked her in the eye. "Do you want the good news or the bad news first?" she asked.

Meg grimaced. *This can't possibly get any worse*, she thought. "I guess I'll take the bad news."

"Well," Roxanne explained, "the bad news is I couldn't get us better seats."

"Really?" Meg asked in mock surprise. "I kind of figured that . . . WHEN I WAS STANDING IN THE LOBBY FOR THE LAST HOUR AND A HALF."

Roxanne stepped back from Meg. "This is a very ugly side of you that I personally am not enjoying."

"Roxanne," Meg said, leaning in and speaking through gritted teeth. "The good news? It'd better be *really* good."

Roxanne was about to explain everything—the good news, the bad news, and what exactly she'd been doing for the last hour and a half—when something stopped her in her tracks.

The concert had ended, kids were pouring out of the convention hall, and in the midst of the crowd Roxanne saw Luke—with Carrie. She nudged Meg and pointed at them.

Meg couldn't believe what she was seeing. Shoving through the crowd was almost impossible, like trying to swim upstream. But somehow, miraculously, through sheer willpower and the help of Roxanne shoving innocent bystanders out of the way, Meg made her way to Luke. Luke saw her coming toward him and waved, not noticing the angry scowl on her face.

"Meg!" Luke said happily. "You're never going to believe what happened!" Meg stood with her arms folded across her chest, waiting for an explanation. "I ran into Carrie on the boardwalk, and she had an extra ticket to the show," Luke continued. "Her dad's a DJ in New York. You won't believe this . . . third row center."

Meg's jaw dropped in utter disbelief. "You saw the Beatles?" she asked slowly, trying to interpret and process exactly what he was saying. "From the third row center?"

"It was a great show. Even better than I thought. When they sang 'Please Please Me' . . . man, was that good," Luke said excitedly. "Don't you feel better now? It all worked out. Now you don't have to feel bad."

Meg looked at him. "Funny," she said sullenly, her voice shaking with jealousy and disappointment. "Right now I couldn't feel worse." She spun around and quickly disappeared into the sea of people making their way outside.

Roxanne chased after her. After thanking Carrie, Luke followed. They caught up with Meg, who was sitting on a concrete ledge outside the convention hall, her face streaked with tears. Roxanne slid onto the ledge next to her.

"This night has been a huge disaster," Meg cried, her eyes red and nose running. "I got in a car accident. Luke's with some other girl. I missed the whole show. I've said every lie in the book to my dad"—Meg glanced at her watch—"who I need to call right now or I'll be grounded until I'm thirty-five. And all for what?" Luke approached them tentatively. "I didn't get to see the Beatles," Meg went on. "Being stuck in the lobby—it was worse than staying home."

"Stuck in the lobby?" Luke asked quietly. Roxanne shook her head, warning Luke not to press for more information.

"I know it seems horrible, Meg," Roxanne

responded sympathetically. "But my good news? I didn't get a chance to tell you in there. . . ."

Meg used her sleeve to dry her tears. "What?" she asked. Her expectations were at an all-time low.

"The Lafayette Motor Inn," Roxanne replied. "On North Carolina Avenue."

"What about it?" Meg asked, her voice weary. She was suddenly exhausted, drained, and absolutely starving.

"It's where the Beatles are staying," Roxanne said, smiling. "And where we're going."

"How on earth do you know that?" Luke asked Roxanne skeptically.

Roxanne shrugged innocently. "Their manager."

Luke didn't buy it. "I have a hard time believing the Beatles' manager would let you in on that little secret."

"It's top secret," Roxanne admitted. She cocked her head to one side and smiled. "I can be very convincing."

"You made out with their manager?" gasped Meg.

Roxanne flipped her hair and smoothed down her dress. "It got us on *Bandstand,* didn't it?" she reminded Meg. Reaching into her purse, she grabbed a tube of lipstick and fixed her smudges.

"Now we're gonna go do something ten times better than hearing the Beatles. . . ." She smacked her lips together and smiled, incredibly satisfied with herself. "We're going to meet them."

Ten

"**I** hate to tell you, Roxanne," Luke told her, breaking the news as gently as possible, "but this guy is not the Beatles' manager."

Luke, Roxanne, and Meg were standing among a growing mob of Beatles fans outside the Lafayette Motor Inn. They were so close to the ocean Meg could taste the salt in the air. If it weren't for the roar created by the hundreds of kids gathering in the hotel driveway awaiting the Beatles' arrival, she'd be able to hear the sound of the surf pounding on the shore.

She thought of all the nights during all those summers down at the shore when she and Roxanne would stay up late and sneak out to the edge of the ocean. They'd wrap themselves in blankets and always say they were going to wait for the sunrise. But to this day they'd still never made it all night. Usually they got too cold or tired and went inside. Earlier in the summer Meg's family had gone down to the shore, but she and

Roxanne had been fighting, so they never got an opportunity to wait for the sunrise. At the rate this night was going, Meg would be lucky if she was home before then.

As excited as Meg was to meet the Beatles, especially because she'd seen so little of their concert, she couldn't help but wish for a simpler time, when lying and deceiving her parents didn't have to be a way of life. Of course, she realized there had been deception on those nights by the water, when her parents thought she and Roxanne were tucked in asleep on the sofa bed. However, sitting fifty feet from her parents' vacation rental seemed substantially different from borrowing her dad's car, lying about her destination, and getting in a car accident.

Outside the hotel the mob was quickly doubling, and Meg was being shoved out of the way by obsessive Beatles fans trying to finagle a closer spot. The packed crowd and the pushing and the yelling were starting to be too much for Meg. So was Luke and Roxanne's incessant bickering.

"This is Brian—Brian Epstein," insisted Roxanne. She was standing next to the guy she'd made out with for over an hour backstage at the Beatles show.

Luke scoffed. "You're kidding, right?" he asked. "Roxanne, you can't be that naive."

Roxanne pulled Brian toward Luke. "Brian, tell them. You're their manager," Roxanne prompted him.

"I'm their manager," Brian said. He shrugged unconvincingly. "I discovered them." Meg raised her eyebrows. *He discovered the Beatles?* she thought. She didn't quite believe this guy. She looked around, aware that the crowd was moving in on her.

"Fine, Roxanne. You're right," Luke conceded. "The Beatles' manager is a guy named Brian Epstein." But he added, "Who's at least thirty years old." Luke looked Roxanne's companion up and down. "And you're, what? Eighteen, tops?"

Roxanne took a good, hard look at the guy she was convinced was the Beatles' manager and gasped, realizing her common sense may have been clouded by the prospect of getting to meet the Beatles. The expression on her face quickly changed from excitement to horror as it occurred to her that she had been used. In a sudden movement she swung her purse and hit him squarely in the shoulder.

"Roxanne!" Meg yelled, trying to stop her. Brian backed up, looking a little frightened of Roxanne's manic state.

She continued to pummel him with her purse. "I . . ." *Whack!* "Made . . ." *Whack!* "Out with you!" *WHACK!* Luke yanked her purse away from her as Brian dived into the sea of people in a rush to escape Roxanne's angry wrath.

"Roxanne, stop!" Luke yelled. "You've made out with tons of guys. What're you getting so upset about?"

Roxanne wrenched her arm free. "I'm not upset that I made out with someone," she spit back. "I'm upset because he was my key to meeting Ringo."

Luke rolled his eyes. "Are you ever not thinking about yourself?" he muttered.

Roxanne looked at him, shocked by his harshness. "I'm doing this for Meg!" she said indignantly. "If I get to meet Ringo too, so what?"

"Really? For Meg?" Luke asked unbelievingly. "Because we wouldn't have to be chasing down the Beatles if you'd just stayed in the concert instead of making her wait in the lobby."

"This coming from a guy who ditched us for some girl in a bikini!" Roxanne reminded him, her voice rising.

"You *gave* away my ticket!" Luke said defensively.

"So the truth comes out," Roxanne said. "You *were* upset."

"Who wouldn't be upset?" Luke asked. "I'm the one who got us those tickets in the first place."

"Well, why didn't you say something?" Roxanne yelled.

"I didn't want to ruin her birthday!" Luke yelled back, feeling attacked. On the curb a group of teenage boys pushed over a car. The sound of windows breaking and people screaming made Meg practically jump out of her skin as her mind flashed back to the riot. It was happening again.

"Meg?" Luke asked, suddenly very concerned. "You're shaking."

Roxanne grabbed her arm. "Meg, what's wrong?"

"I have to go," Meg said, pushing her way out of the crowd, running back toward the car. Luke and Roxanne ran after her.

"I'm sorry," Meg cried, weaving in and out of the crowd of rowdy teenagers. "I just can't do this." Luke and Roxanne followed on both sides.

Suddenly all Meg wanted to do was be home in Philly, safe and sound in her bedroom with the sheets pulled over her head. She wanted it all to be over. The lies, the driving, the Beatles—everything. "I'm sorry, Rox. Even if I met the Beatles, I probably wouldn't enjoy it now," she said.

Just then a limo pulled around the corner and

into the hotel driveway. Meg, Luke, and Roxanne stopped suddenly so they wouldn't get hit.

One by one, four familiar guys got out of the car.

"Are you sure you don't want to meet them?" Roxanne asked. "Because now might be our chance."

Luke sighed, looking at his watch. "Roxanne, let's just go. This has gone on long enough."

"It's up to Meg," Roxanne said. She shrugged.

Meg watched as the Beatles were being rushed into the hotel. *We made it this far,* she thought.

As fans rushed the front doors of the hotel and police made a human barricade to block them, Meg looked at Roxanne, saying, "I'd better call my dad."

Luke sighed heavily. *Here we go again*, he thought. For him to have expected that the evening would end there would have been logical, but unrealistic, and more importantly, un-Roxanne. Instead of heading back to Philly, he stood next to Meg at a pay phone as she explained to her dad that they were going to be on their way home soon. "We're just finishing up signing autographs," she said breathlessly.

Across the street a policeman spoke through a megaphone to instruct the crowd. "Everyone step back," he demanded. "You kids need to disperse and go home."

Meg cringed. "The turnout was way bigger than they expected," she told her father.

As Meg assured her dad they were almost done Luke noticed Roxanne was staring off into space. He could practically see the wheels turning in her head, a plan on the verge of hatching. Roxanne looked at him, her eyes lighting up with an idea. "Oh no," Luke said, looking at Roxanne with an impending sense of dread.

She smiled at him. "Oh yes!" she said. As Meg hung up, Roxanne grabbed both their hands. "Come with me."

Fifteen minutes later Roxanne and Meg were walking down the street holding two large bouquets of flowers, one addressed to Paul and the other addressed to Ringo. Luke trailed behind them, the voice of reason.

"This is never going to work, Roxanne," he complained. "Can we just go?"

Roxanne quickened her pace and tightened her grasp around the glass vase of flowers. Meg struggled to keep up.

"Seriously," Luke continued. "You think they're

going to just give us the room number? Just like that?"

"Don't listen to him, Meg," Roxanne instructed. "He's what they call a naysayer." She kept her gaze forward, holding her chin a little higher, as if Luke's doubts and worries were simply bouncing off her, not affecting her in the least.

However, when the hotel concierge explained to Roxanne for the fifth and final time that under no circumstances would they be allowed up to the fourth floor, Luke couldn't help but say, "I told you so."

Meg and Roxanne sat in the hotel lobby, flowers resting on their laps. "I guess Luke was right," Meg said. She shrugged, looking down at the lavish, completely useless bouquet she'd wanted to give to Paul. "This plan was destined to be a failure."

Roxanne turned to Meg. "Failure?" she asked. "You're both kidding, right?"

"What else could you call this?" Luke responded.

"How about a huge success?" Roxanne answered, leaning in. "Meg," she whispered. "The fourth floor?"

"What about it?"

"The lady said the Beatles are on the fourth

floor," Roxanne whispered fiercely. "That means one thing. . . ."

Meg raised her eyebrows. "We're going up?"

"Exactly," Roxanne said. She smiled.

Luke shook his head. "I don't want any part of it."

Roxanne leaned in. "You went to the Beatles concert with another girl, who has legs the length of telephone poles," she reminded him. "You owe Meg."

Luke looked at Meg and smiled, his attitude suddenly shifted. "How can I help?" he asked sweetly.

"Hurry up," Luke whispered through clenched teeth. He was standing guard outside a small broom closet on the first floor of the hotel as patrons walked by, looking at him oddly. He thumbed through *Look* magazine, trying to attract as little attention as humanly possible.

At the sound of voices nearby he squinted to get a better look down the hall. He could see all the way into the hotel lobby, where police were ushering rowdy Beatles fans outside.

"Seriously," he insisted. "The cops are here. We have to go." The door burst open, revealing Meg and Roxanne, dressed as cleaning ladies in matching pink uniforms with white aprons.

Roxanne pushed a cleaning cart out into the hall, and Meg grabbed a large stack of fresh white towels.

"Housekeeping?" Roxanne asked sweetly. Luke looked the girls up and down, shaking his head in sheer wonder.

"Wow," he said, astonished. "You're really going to do it?"

Roxanne smiled. "We didn't come all this way for nothing," she replied.

Meg was anxious to get the whole escapade over with. She'd told her dad they'd be on the road by now. She was cutting it close. "So?" she asked eagerly. "What's the plan?"

"I say we divide and conquer," Roxanne suggested. She wheeled the cart to the elevator and pressed the up button. "I'll take the elevator," she explained, "because of the cart—"

"And I'll take the stairs?" Meg guessed.

Roxanne smiled. "Great minds think alike," she said. The elevator doors opened. "We'll meet on the fourth floor."

"And what if we see a Beatle?" Meg asked quickly as Roxanne wheeled the cart into the elevator. "How will we get each other's attention?"

"Meg," Roxanne answered calmly. "If I see a

Beatle up close, you'll hear me screaming."

"What about me?" Luke asked. "Meg, should I come with you?"

Meg shrugged, still upset about Carrie. "I'm sure there's someone else you'd rather go with," she said pointedly.

"Meg," he pleaded. "Come on, I said I was sorry."

Roxanne reached out and grabbed Luke by the arm, yanking him into the elevator. "You're safer with me," she said as the door closed. Meg looked around, tightening her grip on the towels, and when she was sure no one was looking, she slipped into a nearby doorway and started up the stairs.

By the time she reached the fourth floor, Meg was out of breath, wondering why she didn't just take the elevator with Roxanne. She poked her head out of the door. The hallway wasn't swarming with people, as the hotel lobby had been, but there were definitely press and security in the halls. Meg took a deep breath, trying to look as if she knew what she was doing and thinking about what she was going to say if she met a Beatle. She walked down the hallway, past the elevator. It looked like it was between the second and third floors. She hoped Roxanne would be up any minute to tell her what to do next.

"Can I have a few of those?" a voice asked. Meg spun around. A man was poking his head out of his hotel room door. Meg gulped when she realized who it was. She was standing right in front of Paul McCartney.

"Wh—what?" she stammered, completely starstruck.

"Extra towels," he said. Meg noticed his hair was wet.

"Come on, you guys," someone shouted from down the hall. "The screening's about to start."

"Screening?" Meg asked blankly.

"*Hard Day's Night*," Paul said with a wink, taking a couple of towels off the top. Meg's eyes widened in disbelief. The movie hadn't even opened in theaters yet. And before she could say anything else, he shut the door. She stood, frozen, completely shell shocked. She'd just come face-to-face with Paul McCartney, the love of her life (besides Luke), and she'd barely managed to stammer out two words. She hit her forehead with the palm of her hand, hoping to knock some sense into herself. One door separated her from Paul. He was on the other side, using her towels. She wondered where Roxanne was. Surely she'd know what to do.

Summoning her courage, she balled her hand

into a tight fist and knocked on his door. "House-keeping," she squeaked, her voice cracking a little. Once again Paul opened the door. Before she could get another word out to Paul, before she even knew what was happening, a man was behind her.

"Can I see some identification, miss?" he asked.

Meg spun around, coming face-to-face with hotel security. "I'm . . . I'm sorry?" she stammered, even more nervous than before. The security guard saw right through her.

"I'm sorry for the disturbance, Mr. McCartney," the man apologized. "Some kids have no respect." Meg's face reddened as Paul smiled at her and shut the door. "Miss," the guard said angrily. "You're coming with me."

Humiliated, Meg followed the security guard back toward the stairs, away from Paul McCartney. As Meg walked by the elevator she didn't notice that it was still between the second and third floors. All she knew was that her face was burning with embarrassment.

"This is all your fault!" Roxanne yelled. She and Luke had been stuck in the elevator for more than ten minutes, which felt like an eternity in such a small space.

"My fault?" Luke asked. "If it were up to me, we'd be back in Philly by now. I'm not the one dressed in a maid's outfit, pushing a cleaning cart!"

"You're the one who pressed that button!" she reminded him.

"It was the button for the fourth floor," he defended himself. "And you told me to press it."

"I didn't know it was going to stop the elevator!" Roxanne shot back.

"Don't start, Roxanne," Luke warned her. He pressed random buttons, hoping to make something happen. "I think I'm claustrophobic."

"I don't even know what that means," Roxanne said.

"Are the walls closing in on us?" Luke asked.

Roxanne looked at him and rolled her eyes. "You have serious problems," she said.

Infuriated, Luke narrowed his eyes. "No kidding." He sat down to wait. "My biggest one is about five feet tall with brown hair and a really big mouth." Roxanne glared at him and slowly sank to the floor.

An hour later Meg was absolutely panicked. She had no idea where Roxanne and Luke were, and there was no way she was going to be allowed back up to the fourth floor. Security was watching her like a hawk as she waited in the lobby. She'd already walked back to the car and checked the lobby bathrooms and the cleaning supply room. Since the cart was still missing, she assumed Roxanne and Luke had successfully made it upstairs. She pictured them sitting in Ringo's hotel room watching *A Hard Day's Night,* while once again she sat in a lobby all alone, waiting.

She looked at her watch. It was well past eleven, and she didn't dare call home. She hoped, if she was lucky, her parents would already be asleep, but Meg knew the chances of their not waiting up were slim to none. Although they hadn't settled on a curfew for the night, JJ had told Meg if she wasn't home by midnight, he was telling her parents where she was. In less than an hour JJ would be ratting her out. Meg was sure of it. She could just picture the three of them sitting around the kitchen table.

Suddenly Meg's stomach rumbled and growled. Embarrassed, she looked around to see if anyone had heard. She stood up and approached the front desk. Luckily the previous woman's shift had ended, so the new woman knew nothing of botched flower deliveries or cleaning crew disguises.

Meg asked, "Is there anywhere in the hotel I

could buy food?" She realized she hadn't eaten since she left the house that morning. And she was certain that one bowl of Cheerios wasn't going to be enough to get her through the rest of the night.

The woman smiled. "There's a vending machine on the second floor. Turn right when you get off the elevator, and it's at the end of the hallway."

Meg thanked her and walked toward the elevator unnoticed by security. She pressed the button and waited. And waited. And waited. When the elevator never came, she opted once again for the stairs.

Meanwhile, Roxanne and Luke still sat stuck between two floors, wondering when, if ever, they were going to get out of there. Luke had spent a good portion of the last hour listening to all the reasons why—in Roxanne's opinion—Meg should have dumped Luke months ago.

"I mean, I'm the one you have to thank for all this in the first place," Roxanne pointed out.

"Being stuck in an elevator?" Luke asked. "Yeah, don't hold your breath waiting for that thank-you note."

"I'm talking about Meg," Roxanne said. "I'm the one who got her to admit she had feelings for you. If it wasn't for me, she'd still just see you as the slightly geeky, annoying guy in the record store."

"I'm sorry," Luke said sarcastically. "What part of this conversation am I supposed to be thanking you for?"

Roxanne sighed, exasperated. "All I'm trying to tell you," she responded, "is that when it comes to the ways of women, you're pretty out of it." Luke looked at her blankly. "Okay, you're *really* out of it."

"Is this about Carrie?" Luke asked, finally starting to get it.

"Exactly," Roxanne answered, patting him on the back.

Luke shook his head. "Meg had no right to get so mad. I didn't do anything wrong."

"Girls don't need a reason to get mad," Roxanne explained. "They just do."

"Then, girls are crazy."

"Now you're getting it." Roxanne smiled.

"So assuming we ever get out of this elevator," Luke said, "how am I supposed to get her *un*-mad?"

"You have to give her what she wants," Roxanne answered.

Luke threw his hands in the air, exasperated. "How am I supposed to know what she wants if she doesn't tell me?"

Roxanne sat down next to him. "All girls want the

same thing. Then they don't worry if there are a thousand Carries swarming around you, because they know how you feel. Girls want to hear those three magic words."

"The elevator's moving," Luke said.

Roxanne punched him in the arm. "I love you, you moron!" she yelled. "The three magic words are 'I love you.'"

"Roxanne," Luke answered, "I know. But the elevator . . . it's moving." Roxanne looked up and realized they were heading back down to the first floor.

When Meg got to the vending machine, she had a hard time deciding what she wanted. She was so hungry and thirsty that everything looked good. After careful deliberation she settled on a Coca-Cola and a pack of tutti-frutti gum, figuring the soda would keep her awake and the gum would last the whole drive home. It was no Philly cheesesteak, but for now it would have to do. Meg reached into her purse, trying to find some spare change.

A man came up behind her, patiently waiting his turn. Although she didn't turn around, his presence made her even more nervous. She dug around, her fingers searching for the familiar feel of the coins, finding nothing. She began to search more fervently.

And then she remembered. She was broke. Every last cent had been spent on those stupid flowers. She didn't have a penny to her name. And suddenly it all felt like too much.

She angrily banged her fist against the machine.

"I can't believe this," she spit, emphasizing each word. "You've got to be kidding!" *Can't anything go right?* she thought. *Is it too much to ask to have a nickel for some soda and gum?* Meg broke down crying. All the stress that the trip was supposed to alleviate—the stress of the riot, of getting in trouble, of worrying about Sam—had only caused her anxiety to double.

"Excuse me," the man behind her said. "Miss?"

"I can't believe this day," she sobbed as she leaned against the vending machine, ranting. "This was supposed to be fun. But now Luke and Roxanne are nowhere to be found, I missed the entire Beatles concert, I got humiliated in front of Paul McCartney, dragged out by hotel security, my brother's gonna rat me out, and my dad is literally going to kill me. And all I wanted was a stupid pack of gum and I can't even do that right because I spent the little amount of money I had on flowers for the Beatles that we weren't even allowed to deliver."

"It's okay," the man said. "We get too many flowers as it is." Meg spun around upon hearing his familiar British accent and came face-to-face with John Lennon.

"Oh my gosh," she sputtered. "You're—you're—"

He held out his hand, revealing a quarter. "Here, to buy you whatever you want," he said with a smile. "Gum and sodas are on me."

Meg smiled, overwhelmed, as he put the money into the machine and handed her a pack of tutti-frutti gum.

Eleven

"**I** can't believe you were stuck in the elevator," Meg said as they crossed over the state line, back into Pennsylvania. Luke drove, going over sixty miles per hour in an attempt to get Meg home before one in the morning. Roxanne and Meg gabbed in the backseat as he drove.

"I can't believe you got John Lennon's autograph," Roxanne answered. "Meg, you're my idol."

Meg smiled proudly. She couldn't believe that after a week of bad luck she was holding a napkin with John Lennon's name scrawled on it. Finally her luck had turned. Meg was convinced of that, even as they drove back into Philadelphia, even as she dropped Luke and Roxanne off at their homes, and even as she pulled into her driveway, taking special care not to collide with the mailbox. But when Meg got out of the car, she was confronted by Patty, wrapped in a blanket, waiting on the swings in the backyard. In an instant all her confidence was gone.

"Where have you been?" Patty asked.

"None of your business," Meg said, closing the car door as quietly as possible. "Are Mom and Dad still up?"

Patty didn't beat around the bush. "Where's the autograph?" she asked.

"What?" Meg asked, panicked. She had completely forgotten that the autograph was part of the deal.

Patty stood up, arms folded in front of her chest. The blanket hung over her shoulders like a witch's cape, which Meg thought was fitting.

"John Lennon's autograph?" Patty insisted. "You give it to me, I won't tell Mom and Dad where you've been." Meg's heart sank. Her one happy memory of the night, and it was going to go to Patty. But a promise was a promise and blackmail was blackmail, so Meg knew she had no choice. Reluctantly she reached in her purse and pulled out the napkin. Patty snatched it out of her hand.

"Patty!" Meg snapped.

"What?" asked Patty. "It's mine." She unfolded the napkin and saw the autograph. She stepped back, stunned. "Wow."

Meg nodded sadly. "You happy now?"

Patty smiled. Clenching the napkin tightly in the

palm of her hand, she started to walk down the driveway.

"Where're you going?" Meg asked.

Patty turned. "Oh, Mom and Dad and JJ are in the kitchen. I don't want to get caught. Unfortunately, I think you already have been." And with that, Patty was gone. Meg felt the ball of guilt in the pit of her stomach grow even heavier. It was so heavy, in fact, she almost couldn't bring herself to walk in through the mudroom door. But when she did, and saw her parents and JJ all sitting around the kitchen table with somber expressions, Meg knew it had happened: JJ had ratted her out.

Meg knew in that moment she could kiss everything she loved good-bye—*Bandstand*, Luke, Roxanne. She was certain of only one thing—if she didn't come up with the best excuse of her life, she was a goner. She really wished she hadn't dropped Roxanne off before coming home. Roxanne surely would have been able to come up with a great lie.

"It's all in the details," Roxanne had once explained. "The specifics." Meg wished that she'd asked Roxanne for a just-in-case lie before she'd hopped out of the car.

"I can explain—" Meg began, desperate to counter anything JJ had told her parents.

"I don't want to hear it, Meg," Jack snapped, his brow furrowed, wrinkles etched permanently on his forehead. "Not now."

"But Dad," Meg protested.

"I said quiet!" Jack demanded. Helen broke down crying. Self-consciously she brushed past Meg and hurried upstairs. Meg heard the bedroom door slam. Jack gave JJ a long, frustrated look and headed after his wife.

Meg stood frozen. She felt as if she were sinking in quicksand. Everything around her was going wrong, and every time she tried to worm her way out of trouble, she sank deeper into it. She couldn't believe it was happening again. How much trouble could one sixteen-year-old get into? But instead of taking responsibility for her actions and subsequent mistakes, she found it easier to blame JJ. "I can't believe you," Meg spit at her brother. "I thought we had a deal."

"This isn't about you, Meg," JJ muttered.

Meg didn't believe a word he said anymore. "You just sell me out so you can look good to Mom and Dad. That way they think I'm the screwup, while you get to do whatever you want, go wherever you want, with whomever you want, while I'm stuck here, in this house . . ."

"I got my orders," JJ mumbled under Meg's rant. When he realized she hadn't heard him, he raised his voice. "I'm leaving, Meg. For Parris Island."

"Parris Island?" Meg repeated. She had no idea what JJ was talking about.

He explained. "In South Carolina. Boot camp."

Meg looked at her brother, and suddenly everything else—which two seconds ago had mattered more than anything—just slipped away. The riot, the hop, the accident, the concert— suddenly none of it mattered, because it was official: JJ was leaving.

He wouldn't be an hour away at school, coming home on the weekends to do his laundry and give Meg a hard time about dating. Her brother would be gone, in the marines, in South Carolina, and maybe, if there was a war, he'd end up somewhere even farther away than that.

Meg finally understood. Her dad's stern look wasn't his considering how to punish her. Her mom's tears weren't because Meg had disappointed them yet again. It was because suddenly JJ's enlisting was real. JJ was shipping out, first thing in the morning. By lunchtime the next day he'd be long gone. A wave of sadness washed over Meg.

"Oh, JJ," she said. Stunned, she sat down at the

kitchen table. "What am I going to do without you here?"

"I covered for you, ya know," JJ said, sitting down next to Meg. "With Dad."

She wasn't expecting that. "Really?"

"You got lucky this time, Meg," JJ said. "Next time you might not be."

"What am I going to do without you?" Meg asked again, near tears.

JJ thought for a moment. "Come on," he said, putting his shoes on and heading for the mudroom door.

"Wait!" Meg grabbed her brother's arm to stop him. "Where are we going?"

"No questions," he demanded.

Meg relented. "Fine. On one condition." She held out the car keys. "You drive." JJ reached out and took them, happy to oblige.

Meg and JJ lay on the hood of the car, looking up at the sky full of stars. They were parked on a hillside a few miles outside the city, and the stars twinkled brighter than ever. A train track ran through a shallow valley down below. JJ and Meg stared into the night above them.

"Is it too late for a wish?" Meg asked.

"Only on the first star," JJ reminded her. They always used to wait in the backyard for the first star and try to beat the other one to it, fighting over who got the wish, as if there were a finite number of wishes, not quite enough to go around.

As she scanned the sky for the Big Dipper, Meg pondered, "So many stars . . . doesn't it make you feel . . ." She searched for the right word.

"Small? Insignificant?" JJ offered. Meg's stomach growled. "Hungry for a cheesesteak?" her brother joked.

Meg smiled. "Yeah," she said thoughtfully. "Especially that part about the cheesesteak."

"So," JJ said. "Was the concert fun?"

Meg shrugged. "I wouldn't know, I only saw one song."

JJ sat up. "What?"

"Long story," Meg said, shaking her head.

"So all that lying?" JJ said. "It was for nothing?"

Meg sighed. "I guess so." But as she said the words she realized she didn't quite feel that way. Surrounded by darkness and the hum of the crickets, Meg closed her eyes and thought about the adventure she'd had. It may not have been perfect, but it all was definitely worth it.

Suddenly a train roared by. Meg and JJ jumped

off the hood and ran for the tracks as soon as it had passed. They each carried a large flashlight, and the light bounced off the steel of the rails as Meg and JJ searched between the tracks.

"Over here!" Meg yelled happily. She reached down and picked up a flattened penny. JJ shone his light in her direction. The penny seemed to sparkle in her hand as the light reflected off of it. The rumble of another train could be heard in the distance. As Meg hopped off the tracks JJ kept searching, looking for another penny.

As the train roared closer Meg ran up the hill, anxious to get plenty of distance from the tracks below. "JJ! Hurry!" she yelled as her brother continued to look for the other coin. The lights of the train rounded the corner below the hillside.

"JJ!" Meg cried, afraid for her brother. *Why isn't he leaving the tracks?* she thought frantically. As the train barreled down on him, closer and closer, JJ saw the penny, wedged under the track. He reached down to grab it.

"JJ!" Meg shrieked, terror-stricken and shaking, sure her brother would be crushed.

Quickly JJ pocketed the penny and hopped off the tracks, moments before the train whizzed by, still close enough to feel the sheer force of it. And suddenly it was quiet again. JJ looked up at Meg, satisfied with himself.

She came running down the hill and plowed right into him, tackling him to the ground. "What were you thinking?" she cried, her eyes full of tears of fear, anger, and relief. She pummeled his chest with her fists. He pushed her off him and sat up, opening his fist, revealing a matching smashed penny.

"For luck," he said. "I just wanted to make sure it worked." He winked at her. "Where we're going, we're both gonna need it." Meg looked at her brother in absolute disbelief. Exhausted, she fell back into the grass, surrounded by the twinkling stars and the night sky, wondering how much luck her penny would be able to give.

Twelve

Meg stepped off the bus, then paused on the curb and looked up at the indigo sky, taking in the magic hour—that in-between moment of every day when the sun has just set and day becomes night. As Meg walked alone down the familiar Philly street for the first time since the riot, she realized she had changed. Although Meg couldn't point to anything tangible to prove it, inside she felt different. Inside she *was* different.

As she walked past buildings and storefronts she'd passed hundreds of times she felt a sense of gratitude. The last few weeks had been fraught with challenges and difficulties. She'd done things she was proud of, things she'd regretted. But after everything, she realized that even if her father grounded her a hundred times, she had something inside of her that couldn't be diminished. She'd had a taste of freedom. And although she had gone about it all wrong, and everything that could have gone wrong did, it was still worth it (save for getting caught).

The riot had changed her. Meg had lost her childlike sense of invincibility the moment the first brick smashed through her dad's store window. And she was scared. Scared of going back out into a world where people were so angry that they could tear down neighborhoods and burn buildings to the ground, where they could inflict pain and suffering on one another, where they could make her feel like her friendship with Sam was wrong.

Still, she felt lucky to have Sam as a friend, in spite of it all. Not to mention Luke and Roxanne— their birthday gift had come at just the right time, just when she needed her friends the most. Granted, their execution was misguided at times, but they truly wanted her to have the most memorable birthday ever. And after seeing people shot and beaten in the riot, after being caught in the middle of the madness and mayhem, she knew that having the freedom to get out of town, to dance to music she loved, and to see the concert of her dreams made her the luckiest girl alive.

Although things hadn't gone as planned, it had been enough. She'd felt what it was like to hop in the car, roll down the window, step on the gas pedal, and take off for the unknown, where absolutely anything could happen. With wind on her face, her hair flying behind her, she had grasped the steering wheel with both hands, experiencing a sense of freedom and control she'd never imagined. Finally feeling as though, for good or bad, she was in control, and no matter how many road bumps she encountered, in the end, just like with the riot, just like with this trip, it all would be okay.

As kids played stickball in the street, Meg walked around them, careful not to interrupt their game. She reached into her pocket and pulled out her flattened penny, feeling sure that she finally had luck on her side. She smiled, thinking of the night on the train tracks with JJ. She missed him already and wondered if the sun had set yet in South Carolina. Maybe it was already dark. Maybe JJ was looking for the first star, hoping to make a wish.

Meg turned her face toward the sky and looked around, scanning the sky for that first twinkling star. Tilting her head all the way back, she saw it— the first star of the night. High above her, it looked closer than it really was. She closed her eyes tightly, scrunching up her face in thought for a moment, and then quickly ran down the staircase leading to the Vinyl Crocodile. When she looked past Luke into the listening booth, she realized that tonight's wish had come true: Sam was there.

As she headed for the booth Luke stepped in front of her, catching her off guard. "Meg," he said, grabbing her arm. She was still giving him a bit of the cold shoulder from the other night.

"Luke," she said. "I was just going to see—"

"Sam," he interrupted. "I know." Nervously he took a deep breath.

"What's wrong?" Meg asked. "Are you okay?"

Luke nodded. "I should have said this weeks ago," he said. "Hell, months ago. I've been wanting to say it forever, but . . . I don't know. I guess I've never said it before." Meg stared at him, unsure of what was coming.

"Meg," he said, looking into her blue eyes. "I love you." Meg smiled. Her whole body felt warm and tingly. She looked into his eyes and could see her reflection in them, again and again.

"I love you too," she said.

Meg slid into a seat next to Sam in the listening booth. He looked up, surprised, and quickly took off his headphones.

"So . . . ?" Meg asked, as if they were in mid-conversation.

"So what?" he asked, the music still playing from the headphones around his neck. Meg could hear the chorus to "Catch the Wind."

"So . . . are we?" she said. "Are we friends or not?"

Sam looked her squarely in the eyes. "You really need to ask?"

Meg shrugged innocently, wilting under his gaze. "I didn't think I had to . . . but then we got in that stupid argument. And then the riot happened. And my uncle . . . he just . . ." Her voice sank to an almost inaudible whisper. "He left you there."

"You think because of that I wouldn't want to be friends anymore?" Sam asked.

"You didn't want to be friends over a lot less than that," Meg pointed out. They both knew she was referring to their fight about the citywide curfew.

Sam looked down at his hands. He clearly had a lot on his mind. There was so much he could have said in that moment. He looked at Meg, sitting there next to him, her hair pulled back into a mass of blond curls, wearing her light yellow blouse and a skirt he'd never seen before. He thought of how hard things always seemed but how easy it felt with Meg. How when he was with her, the world just felt right. He wanted to tell her how badly he felt about their fight, how happy he'd been when she showed up at the Girard store, how worried he'd been that he wouldn't be able to protect her in the riot, and how abandoned he'd felt when her uncle took her away. There was so much he wanted to say.

"I passed," he said modestly. "The driving part."

Meg clapped her hands together, excited. "I knew it!" she exclaimed happily. "Do you have your license?" she asked.

Sam reached into his pocket and pulled his license out. He shrugged. "Seems silly to have a license without a car, but . . ." He handed it to her. Meg smiled at the picture. Sam looked so proud, a huge grin on his face, smiling from ear to ear.

"It's perfect," Meg said, a hint of jealously in her voice.

"Let's see yours," Sam said.

Meg shook her head. "No way," she responded. "It's terrible." Sam gave her a look, and cracking under his gaze, Meg relented. "Okay, but if you tell me it's fine, I'm leaving." She reluctantly handed Sam her license.

Sam pulled the picture closer, inspecting it carefully. Meg was right, it wasn't the best picture— but not because of her hair or her smile or any of the things she was complaining about. It was her eyes. They looked sad and hollow, like she'd just lost her best friend.

"You were upset . . . ," Sam said. "In this picture. Right?" Meg shrugged a yes. "Why?" he asked. "You'd just passed your test. You worked so hard for that."

"We worked so hard together," Meg said, correcting him. "When I saw you, I felt like . . . I don't know." She shrugged, feeling like she was saying too much, things she'd only thought of in her head but had never articulated.

"When you saw me, you what?" he asked.

"It was just like in the riot," she replied. "You were right there, right next to me, but you felt so far away." Meg took a deep breath, feeling both uncomfortable and relieved at the same time. Her heart had felt so heavy for so long with thoughts and feelings she couldn't express. Finally she had a chance. "When Pete pulled me away from you," she continued, "it felt . . . it felt like what always happens. Whether it's kids at school or like that night with the police or a mean lady in a diner who won't seat us or my uncle or our dads . . . people are constantly pulling us away from each other." She stopped. After a moment Meg asked the question she'd wanted to ask that day when she went to the

Girard store to see Sam. "Sometimes I feel like no one wants us to be friends, and it scares me because I'm afraid that maybe you feel the same way."

Sam nodded, a small smile forming across his face. After a moment he reached down and pulled out a small bag overflowing with tissue paper.

"This is for you," he said. "Happy birthday, Meg."

Meg smiled, surprised. She riffled the tissue paper and looked in the bottom of the bag. "What is this?" she asked as she pulled out two tickets.

"*A Hard Day's Night,*" Sam explained. "The movie."

"You're kidding," Meg said. She smiled. She hadn't even told Sam about the Beatles concert and Atlantic City and everything in between.

"I know you love the Beatles," Sam added. "I wanted to get you tickets to the concert in Philly, but—"

"It was sold out?" Meg guessed.

Sam nodded and then quickly added, "I gave you two. In case you wanted to ask Roxanne or Luke or someone."

"Thank you, Sam," she said. "I love it. I can't wait to see it."

Sam grinned proudly, happy that he'd given Meg something he knew she'd wanted badly—two uninterrupted hours watching the Beatles.

"And I do want to ask someone," Meg added, rubbing her penny between her fingers for luck. "I want to ask you."

Sam was taken aback. He looked down nervously at his hands, fumbling with the headphones. Shyly he said, "I think I'm free."

Meg nodded, handing Sam his ticket. "Yeah," she said. "Me too."

The American Dreams "Dreams Come True" Sweepstakes Official Rules

NO PURCHASE NECESSARY TO ENTER OR WIN.
Void wherever prohibited or restricted by law.

Limit one entry per person for the Sweepstakes period. Not responsible for: late, lost, stolen, damaged, undelivered, mutilated, illegible, or misdirected entries; postage due; or typographical errors in the rules. Entries void if they are in whole or in part illegible, incomplete, or damaged. No facsimiles, mechanical reproductions or forged entries. Sweepstakes starts on May 1, 2004 and all entries must be postmarked January 15, 2005, and received by January 21, 2005 (the "Sweepstakes period").

All entries become the property of Simon & Schuster Inc. and will not be acknowledged or returned.

Simon & Schuster Inc. will choose one (1) winner in a random drawing consisting of all eligible entries received, and will award one (1) Grand Prize to an eligible U.S. or Canadian entrant.

Grand Prize Winners will be eligible for a chance for a walk-on role on the NBC Series "American Dreams" (the "Series"). All details of the walk-on role to be determined by Sponsors, in Sponsors' sole discretion, subject to availability and production exigencies. Winners must be available during the Series' production schedule and on the dates selected by Sponsors. Grand Prize includes round-trip coach air transportation for 4 (at least one person must be 18 years or older) from a major airport nearest the winner's residence to Los Angeles, CA, hotel accommodations in Los Angeles (2 standard rooms, double occupancy) for 3 days and 2 nights, ground transportation to and from the airport to the hotel, and a visit to the NBC set of the television series "American Dreams," provided that the show is in production during winner's trip. Prize does not include transfers, gratuities, upgrades, personal incidentals, meals or any other any expenses not specified or listed herein. Total retail value of Grand Prize: approximately $4,000. All travel subject to availability. Restrictions and blackout dates may apply. Sponsors reserve the right to substitute a similar prize of equal or greater value at their sole discretion. Travel and hotel arrangements to be determined by the Sponsors. The Sponsors in their sole discretion reserve the right to provide ground transportation in lieu of air transportation.

One (1) Grand Prize winner will be selected at random from all eligible entries received in a drawing to be held on or about January 22, 2005. Winner will be allowed to choose 3 people to accompany him/her on the Grand Prize trip, at least one travel companion must be the winner's parent or legal guardian. Any other minor travel companions must also be accompanied by their parent or legal guardian. The Grand Prize winner must be able to travel during the months of February 2005 through April 2005. If the Grand Prize winner is unable to travel on the dates specified by the Sponsors, then prize will be forfeited and awarded to an alternate winner. In the event that the show American Dreams is cancelled, postponed or delayed for any reason, or if any prize component is not available for any reason, then Sponsors will only be responsible for awarding the remaining elements of the prize which shall constitute full satisfaction of the Sponsors prize obligation to winner & no substitute or additional compensation will be awarded. Winner will be notified by U.S. mail and by telephone, within 15 days of the random drawing. Any notification/prize that is returned as undeliverable will result in an alternate winner being chosen. Odds of winning depend on the number of eligible entries received. Sweepstakes is open to legal residents of the continental U.S. (excluding Alaska, Hawaii, Puerto Rico, and Guam) and Canada (excluding Quebec) ages 8–16 as of March 1, 2004. Proof of age is required to claim prize. If winner is a minor, then prizes will be awarded in the name of the winner's parent or legal guardian. Void wherever prohibited or restricted by law. All provincial, federal, state, and local laws apply. Employees of Simon & Schuster Inc., National Broadcasting Company, Inc., ("NBC") (collectively, the "Sponsors") and their respective suppliers, parent companies, subsidiaries, affiliates, agencies, and participating retailers, and persons connected with the use, marketing, or conducting of this Sweepstakes are not eligible. Family members living in the same household as any of the individuals referred to in the preceding sentence are not eligible. Prizes are not transferable, may not be redeemed for cash, and may not be substituted except by Sponsors, in which case a prize of equal or greater value will be awarded. If the prize is forfeited or unclaimed, if a prize notification is undeliverable, or in the event of non-compliance with any of these requirements, the prize will be forfeited and the Sponsors will randomly select from remaining eligible entries an alternate winner.

If the potential winner is a Canadian resident, then he/she must correctly answer a skill-based question administered by mail. If the potential winner does not correctly answer the skill-based question, then an alternate winner will be selected from all remaining eligible entries.

All expenses on receipt and use of prizes including provincial, federal, state, and local taxes are the sole responsibility of the of the winner's parent or legal guardian. On winner's behalf, winner's parents or legal guardians will be required to execute and return an Affidavit of Eligibility and a Liability/Publicity Release and all other legal documents that the Sweepstakes Sponsors may require (including a W-9 tax form) within 15 days of attempted notification or an alternate winner may be selected. Each travel companion or travel companion's parent or legal guardian if travel companion is a minor, will be required to execute a liability release form prior to ticketing.

By participating in the Sweepstakes, entrants agree to be bound by these rules and the decisions of the judges and Sponsors, which are final in all matters relating to this Sweepstakes. Failure to comply with these Official Rules may result in disqualification of your entry and prohibition of any further participation in this Sweepstakes. By accepting the prize, the winner's parent or legal guardian grants to Sponsors the right to use his/her name and likeness for any advertising, promotional, trade, or any other purpose without further compensation or permission, except where prohibited by law.

By entering, entrants release Sponsors and their respective divisions, subsidiaries, affiliates, advertising, production, and promotion agencies from any and all liability for any loss, harm, damages, costs, or expenses, including without limitation property damages, personal injury, or death, arising out of participation in this Sweepstakes, the acceptance, possession, use, or misuse of any prize, claims based on publicity rights, rights of privacy, intellectual property rights, defamation, or merchandise delivery.

For the name of the prize winner (available after February 5, 2005) send a separate, stamped, self-addressed envelope to Winners' List, Dreams Come True Sweepstakes, Simon & Schuster Children's Marketing Department, 1230 Avenue of the Americas, New York, New York 10020.

Sponsors: Simon & Schuster Children's Publishing, 1230 Avenue of the Americas, New York, NY 10020; and National Broadcasting Company, Inc., 3400 West Olive Avenue #600, Burbank, CA 91505.